LAYERED LIES

KATHLEEN SUZETTE

Copyright © 2024 by Kathleen Suzette. All rights reserved. This book is a work of fiction. All names, characters, places and incidents are either products of the author's imagination, or used fictitiously. Any resemblance to actual events, locales or persons, living or dead, is entirely coincidental. All rights reserved. No part of this book may be reproduced or transmitted in any form or by any means, electronically or mechanical, without permission in writing from the author or publisher.

Sign up to receive my newsletter for updates on new releases and sales:

https://www.subscribepage.com/kathleen-suzette

Follow me on Facebook:

https://www.facebook.com/Kathleen-Suzette-Kate-Bell-authors-759206390932120

❧ Created with Vellum

CHAPTER 1

"I am starving," my best friend Lucy Gray said as we stood at the counter of the Cup and Bean Coffee Shop. She turned to me. "It's a good thing we're getting a muffin."

I nodded as I paid for our orders. I had gotten a caramel latte, and Lucy had gone with an iced mocha. We both chose a cherry chocolate muffin to go with our coffee. I was a baker, and I recognized a good muffin when I saw it. The Cup and Bean had tasty baked goods, and I wasn't going to pass it up. The muffins had chopped cherries in them and large chunks of chocolate. What could be tastier? My stomach growled at the thought of the muffin. I inhaled the scent of coffee and baked goods before answering. "I'm famished. I should have eaten something before we went on our run."

We grabbed our coffee and muffins and turned to find a table in the packed coffee shop when a woman walked through the front door. She was dressed in a business suit in lime green with navy trim wool, and even though I couldn't see the label from where I stood, I was certain it was Chanel. Our eyes locked, and I realized I recognized that copper-colored hair swept into an updo. She smiled, showing off Hollywood white teeth.

"Allie Blanchard," Penny Braxton said, heading in our direction. "What a coincidence, running into you here. You've been on my mind for weeks now. How are you?"

I forced myself to smile, suddenly aware of my appearance. Lucy and I had gone out for an early morning run and had done some hill work in one of the nicer neighborhoods in Sandy Harbor. My long red hair had plagued me the entire run, with locks slipping out from the high ponytail I had put it into and sweat trickling down my face and back. I didn't need a mirror to know I looked frightful. If there had been a rock to crawl under, I would have done it because Penny Braxton was one of the richest women in town. Her put-together look clashed with my unkempt one.

I smiled in spite of how I looked. "Good morning, Penny, how are you doing? Fancy meeting you here. Lucy and I were just out for our morning run and decided we had better stop in and get some coffee and something to eat." I was relatively certain that Penny would not be buying a full-fat, full-sugar latte and a huge muffin. No, Penny would be sipping on a fat-free, sugar-free latte, and skip the muffin, I was certain.

"Yes, we've been out running," Lucy said, stepping closer to me. "How are you doing, Penny? Haven't seen you around in forever. I love your suit. It's the perfect color for spring."

Penny didn't even glance at Lucy. "I'm doing great, Allie. Listen, you know I have an annual garden party every year, yes? It's the event of the season, and everyone who is anyone will be there."

I nodded. Penny's annual garden party was a party I would never be invited to, but it was the talk of the town every year and it always made the local newspaper. "Yes, I know you have a garden party. I hear it's wonderful." The words were out of my mouth before I had a chance to think them through. I didn't want her to think I was whining about never being invited. I was quite certain that the guests on her invitation list were only the wealthiest and most public image conscious people in town.

She smiled and nodded. "Yes, as I said, my garden party is the event of the year as far as I'm concerned," she chuckled. "I'm sure other people think their events are the events of the year, but they are sadly mistaken." She laughed again and shook her head. "I'm kidding, of course. But I work hard on my garden all year long, and now that it's almost summer, everything is in bloom and on display for all my guests to admire. The garden society will be coming around for the annual judging soon, and you know I intend to win. And, of course, it wouldn't be a garden party without the most delectable food I can lay my hands on. And that's where you come in."

"Oh? What do you mean?" I asked, suddenly feeling giddy. I had a reputation for the finest baked goods in this town, and I had a feeling I was about to be summoned to the great Penny Braxton Spring Garden Party.

"I want something fresh for my dessert choices this year. I've been using a little patisserie over in Bangor, but it seems this year they just have the same old choices they've had for several years now, and that just won't do. I want something fresh and exciting. And when I think about fresh and exciting, I think about your desserts. How would you like to provide the desserts for my garden party?"

"That's right up Allie's alley," Lucy gushed, then grimaced when she realized what she had said.

I inhaled, trying to settle my nerves. I wasn't officially a caterer in any form, but I frequently made desserts for events around town. Everyone knew I could supply the freshest, most amazing desserts imaginable, and being asked to provide desserts for Penny's garden party was exciting.

I took a deep breath. "I would love to supply the desserts for your party. What did you have in mind?"

She shrugged, glancing at the short line at the front counter and checking the time on her watch. "I don't really know yet. I like to have three or four unique items. Why don't you think about it and give me some choices to choose from? I love pie of any kind, but I want something fresh and light. And then some small cookies would be nice, as well as a cake."

I nodded. "Why don't I sit down and think about things, and I can call you with a list of items that I think of?" I winced. I had just repeated what she had said. Why did this woman make me feel so awkward?

She sniffed, turning back to the short line as it shortened even more. "That sounds fantastic. Come up with a list of items and give me a call. Oh, and I am allergic to walnuts, so no walnuts. I get deathly ill."

I nodded. "Duly noted. No walnuts." My mind was

already spinning with ideas. This was a spring garden party and that called for light desserts.

She nodded without looking at me. "Great. I'll talk to you in a couple of days."

"Penny," I said as she glided over to the counter. She stopped and turned to me. "What day is your party?"

"May twenty-fifth."

I nodded. "Sounds great." I glanced at Lucy, and we headed to the corner table, where our friend Mr. Winters sat with his poodle beneath the table, patiently waiting for a treat or a pat on the head.

He looked up from his paper as we sat down. "How goes it?"

I leaned forward. "Penny Braxton just asked me to make the desserts for her garden party," I whispered.

He glanced over at the woman standing in line. "Sounds fine."

"You don't understand, it's *Penny Braxton*," Lucy whispered, emphasizing the name.

He glanced back at Penny again and shrugged. "Okay. Sounds like fun. What kind of dessert are you going to make?"

I shook my head. "I have no idea. I'm thinking about a key lime tart. Key lime always spells spring or summer to me, and I can whip up some of those pretty quickly."

Lucy's eyes were on Penny. "She didn't even say hello to me."

I looked at her. "I know. But she's always like that. I swear, I ran into her at the grocery store six months ago, and she didn't even acknowledge me. And when I say I ran into her, I mean physically ran into her when I turned a corner too quickly. She just walked on like I wasn't even there."

Lucy sat, shaking her head. "Seems like a woman with that much money would have better manners. Wouldn't you think her mother would have taught her better manners?" She took a sip of her coffee and nodded. "This is good. I love iced coffee."

I nodded absently. "I can hardly believe that Penny asked me to make the desserts for her garden party. No walnuts. I've got to remember that."

"You better. If she gets deathly ill from something you made, you'll never hear the end of it." She took a big bite of her muffin and groaned. "This is fantastic. I bet you could make something like this for the party. Cherries are a nice spring and summer fruit, and I bet you could make it a lot better."

"I could. But a muffin isn't quite what she's looking for, I don't think. I have a fantastic chocolate layer cake with a whipped raspberry filling I could make," I said, peeling the liner from my muffin. "Chocolate and raspberry always go together. And I could make the filling with white chocolate. Mix it up a little. Doesn't that sound good?"

"Sounds fantastic. You'll need somebody to sample the cake, won't you?" Mr. Winters asked.

I grinned. "Of course." I glanced beneath the table at the little gray poodle. "How are you doing today, Sadie?" I asked, rubbing her ear. The little dog thumped her tail against the floor excitedly, expecting a treat from me, but I didn't have anything that would be suitable for a dog. "I should've brought you a cookie."

Mr. Winters took a sip of his coffee. "It's okay; she's had a pup cup. The vet says she can't have too many treats, so she's fine."

I nodded and glanced over at Penny as she picked up her iced coffee and headed out the door. As I suspected, she didn't get a muffin or other bakery treat. The woman looked like a model, and I couldn't imagine that she ate many treats, even though she was asking me to make them for her party.

CHAPTER 2

"This is going to be so much fun. I have a lovely floral dress with pink and green flowers I'm going to wear for the garden party," Lucy said as she helped me set ingredients out on my kitchen island. It was two weeks after we had spoken to Penny Braxton at the coffee shop, and I was making my chocolate raspberry layer cake, key lime tartlets, strawberry cheesecake bites, and lemon merengue tiramisu. I was a little nervous if you want to know the truth. Who wouldn't be? Penny was paying me a pretty penny to supply the baked goods for her elegant garden party, pardon the pun. The desserts had to be perfect.

I turned to her. "Oh, that sounds wonderful. I have

a lovely blue and yellow floral dress I'm going to wear. But I wonder if she'll kick us out the back door before we get to see anything?" We needed to be dressed nicely in case we ran into any of her guests, but I wasn't going to hold my breath hoping she would let us hang around for the party.

She turned to me and gasped. "What? What are you talking about?"

I shrugged as I set the baking powder and a bottle of vanilla on the island. "We've never been invited to that party before. Just because I'm making the desserts doesn't mean she's going to allow us to wander around the grounds. It would be nice if she did, but I wouldn't be surprised if she doesn't."

"Yeah, she isn't going to let commoners like the two of you wander around her mansion," Lucy's husband Ed said from the kitchen table. He had shown up early to go golfing with Alec, and they were enjoying a cup of coffee before leaving.

"Ed's right," Alec said as he took a sip of his coffee. "The two of you aren't blue bloods. You'll probably be escorted from the grounds by the guards after you drop the food off."

I eyed him, one eyebrow raised. "Guards? What are you talking about, guards?"

He shrugged innocently. "Don't people like Penny

Braxton have guards? I mean, how do they keep the riffraff off their property otherwise?"

Lucy snorted and set down a mixing bowl. "You two are nuts. There aren't any guards, and we will not be escorted off the property. At least, we better not be. I want to see her garden. Don't you think it has to be absolutely beautiful, Allie?"

I nodded. "I don't doubt that it's the most beautiful garden we've never seen. Because we've never seen it."

Alec chuckled. "And you're probably never going to see it. Just admit it. We are not the Braxtons' cup of tea. Get it? Cup of tea? I bet they're serving tea, aren't they? It's probably this highfalutin, hoity-toity tea party."

Ed nodded. "You know it. They're not serving plain black Folgers coffee there. It's going to be expensive tea from Britain with a bunch of finger sandwiches with cucumbers and grapes."

"You mean cucumbers and cream cheese?" Alec asked.

He nodded. "That's exactly what I meant. Tiny little sandwiches."

Lucy and I looked at each other. "They don't know what they're talking about," I said. "But it occurred to me that she might not allow us to hang out after we deliver the goods."

Lucy sighed. "Then I've wasted a hundred bucks on a new dress."

"A hundred bucks? You spent a hundred bucks on a new dress?" Ed asked, his head whipping around to look at her.

She nodded. "Of course I did. Did you think I was just going to show up at Penny Braxton's house dressed in rags? You didn't even comment on my new hairstyle." She patted the side of her hair. I was impressed because she wasn't going with any wild colors this time around. It was a short blonde bob, and it looked lovely.

"I noticed your hair," I told her, patting her on the shoulder and going to the refrigerator to get the eggs. "It's very pretty."

"I know you noticed it, Allie," she said, giving Ed the eye. "Allie always notices when I do something new with my hair. But Ed, you never notice anything. You should pay more attention."

He shrugged. "Yeah, I probably should, but I probably won't. So don't be surprised. It's nothing personal; I just don't remember to pay attention."

Alec laughed and took another sip of his coffee. "That's going to get you into trouble someday, Ed."

He shook his head. "We've been married for thirty years. If it was going to get me in trouble, it would have gotten me into trouble a long time ago."

"It got you into trouble years ago, but I guess you've forgotten that," Lucy said, sounding miffed. She went to the refrigerator and got some butter out.

"You're right, I forgot," Ed said. "But I still think you're the most beautiful woman in the entire world."

Lucy wasn't going to buy it. Ed rarely complimented her, but I knew that didn't mean he didn't love her. Ed just wasn't the kind of person to fall all over anyone. Although, if he were a smarter man, he would have fallen all over Lucy.

She sighed. "Let's just ignore them, Allie. What do you want me to get started on?"

"I want to get started on the layer cake first, so the layers have plenty of time to cool after we bake them. If you would measure out the flour and sugar, that would be fantastic." I loved a good chocolate cake. I was going to fancy up the frosting and make some flowers to go along with the theme of the garden party. "I can hardly wait to see how everything turns out. The tarts will be perfect with some fresh flowers." I wanted everything to shout spring, and shout they would.

Alec got up and took his empty coffee cup to the sink, rinsed it out, and placed it in the dishwasher. "I guess we'll get going now. You two enjoy yourselves with your baking." He came over and gave me a quick kiss. "And I hope there's going to be extras." One eyebrow shot upward.

I nodded. "I'll make some extras." Alec loved sweets, and he loved my baking.

He kissed me on the side of the cheek. "I knew I married you for a reason."

I looked at him, one eyebrow raised. "Well, if I had known that was the only reason you were marrying me, I would've starved you of desserts."

"It would serve you right," Ed said, rinsing out his coffee cup and putting it in the dishwasher. He sidled up to Lucy. "Can I have a kiss?"

She shook her head. "No. You didn't notice my hair."

He sighed. "Your hair is beautiful, as are you."

Lucy's mouth dropped open. "Wow. What do you want?"

He shrugged. "Nothing."

She gave him a peck on the cheek and stood staring after her husband as the two men left.

"Miracles still happen," I said to her as I got the baking chocolate from the cupboard and got a small bowl to melt it in.

"You're telling me." She measured flour into the large mixing bowl. "Do you really think Penny will make us leave after we deliver the desserts?"

I shrugged as I unwrapped the squares of baking

chocolate. "I hope not. I would love to see what her garden looks like, and I'd love to see the setup for the party. I don't know why she has never invited us to that party."

She frowned. "Really? You don't know why?"

I laughed. "Okay, I know why. We just don't run in her circles. But she seems perfectly nice; it's not like she isn't a nice person. It's just we aren't friends of hers. But maybe after making these desserts, and she and her guests see how good they are, we will become friends." I knew I was stretching the truth. The most we would get is another request for more desserts at next year's party. Or, if everything fell apart, the worst that could happen would be she would tell everybody never to buy desserts from me. I sighed. If that happened, I would be devastated. Even though Penny Braxton was snooty, she had a lot of pull in this town, and the last thing I wanted was to disappoint her and her guests.

Lucy looked at me. "They're going to love the desserts," she said as if reading my mind.

I sighed and smiled. "Of course they are. What's not to love? We have a variety of desserts we're bringing so that everybody will be able to pick what they like best, and there's not a walnut in the bunch."

My black cat, Dixie, sauntered into the kitchen,

stopped, and looked at Lucy, then at me, and yowled plaintively.

"You've already eaten, and none of these treats are for you, mister." Dixie was certain that every time I entered the kitchen and did some cooking or baking, it had to be for him. He was sadly mistaken today.

CHAPTER 3

The following morning, Lucy and I brought the desserts to Penny Braxton's house. Each dessert was carefully packed in pink bakery boxes, and we had dressed up in our lovely floral dresses and high heels. It wasn't often that we got to dress up nicely, and we were excited about this. If there was a chance we would get to linger at the party, I didn't want to feel out of place. And if we showed up in jeans and T-shirts, there was no way Penny was going to allow us anywhere near her guests.

When she opened the door, Penny was dressed in a silk navy blue floral dress that looked expensive. She smiled. "Oh, there you two are. I was beginning to worry."

"I'm so sorry. Are we late?" I asked, wanting to glance at my watch, but my arms were filled with bakery boxes, and there was no way that was going to happen.

She opened the bakery box at the top of the pile in my arms. "These look delectable." She chose a key lime tartlet and closed the lid. "Why don't you take those through the French doors and arrange them on the tables? We are going to set up everything on the tables. Some of my guests have already arrived, but they're early. You know how some people are." She made a face but didn't answer my question about whether or not we were late. She suddenly turned her head and sneezed, wobbling a bit on her heels. "Oh, excuse me. My allergies are acting up. Just what I needed at a garden party."

"Bless you," I said. "Sorry we weren't here a little earlier."

She waved away the thought and headed back to what must have been the kitchen. Although I couldn't see through the doorway, I could hear pots and pans clanking. I glanced at Lucy and shrugged.

"We get to look at the garden," she whispered excitedly.

I nodded as we headed toward the French doors that led from the living room out onto the patio. Before we even got outside, I could see flowering bushes, trees that dripped with flowers, and planters that had all manner of colors and sizes of brightly blooming bushes. I wondered how Penny got everything to bloom at precisely the same time. I looked over my shoulder at Lucy, wide-eyed.

Lucy's eyes were just as wide as mine, and she nodded and whispered, "Wow."

Opening that French door with my arms loaded with bakery boxes was a feat. I had to carefully hold onto them while trying to get one hand close to the doorknob. I turned and turned but couldn't quite get a grip, and there was no place to set the bakery boxes down. I looked at Lucy helplessly.

"You hold my boxes, and I'll open the door."

I shook my head. "No, I can't hold any more bakery boxes. I'll drop them, and then what will we do?" The thought of a heap of fallen bakery boxes filled me with horror. I would never live it down.

"I'll get that for you," a male voice said from behind us.

We both turned to look and saw Penny's husband, Jonathan Braxton, hurrying toward us. He was wearing a white polo shirt and khaki pants. He smiled. "I think I'm going to be the doorman today," he laughed. "I've opened the door at least ten times so far."

I chuckled. "Oh, goodness, I'm so glad that you're

here. I couldn't imagine how I was going to get this door open without some help."

He nodded and pulled the door open wide for us. "No problem. You go on out there and put your boxes down. I heard you were making the desserts, Allie, and I can hardly wait to sink my teeth into them."

"I helped," Lucy said brightly.

He nodded and followed us out onto the patio. There were tiny twinkle lights everywhere, even though it was still daytime. I wondered how long this garden party would last and whether Penny's guests would get to see them twinkle tonight. "I'm sure those desserts are going to be extra tasty because you helped, Lucy."

Lucy giggled like a schoolgirl. "Oh, thank you, Mr. Braxton. That's so kind of you to say."

"Lucy is a great help to me," I said as we set the boxes down on a long table covered in a white tablecloth.

"It's Jonathan. Don't call me Mr. Braxton; that's what you call my father," he said and laughed. Jonathan Braxton was tall and tan with blond hair and perfect teeth.

"Okay, Jonathan," Lucy said, giggling again. "You have such a lovely garden. I've never seen so many flowers in one place before."

She wasn't kidding. We stood for a moment, surveying the plants that flanked the patio.

"Oh, this isn't the garden. This is just the patio area. Penny works on her garden all year long, and it spans a quarter of an acre," he nodded toward a white picket gate about thirty feet from us. I desperately longed to go through that gate, but I wasn't sure I was going to be allowed to do that.

"I'm so impressed," I said. "My husband and I have begun a garden at our house, but it is nowhere near as large as this."

"Well, this took several years to get to this size," he explained. "Not to mention a lot of money." He rolled his eyes and then chuckled. "If you'll excuse me, I need to see if Penny needs some help." He turned and went inside.

"Isn't that lovely?" I said, pointing to some purple flowers on a nearby flowerpot. "I love dark purple flowers like that. It just seems like they always stand out in a garden."

"That's Wolfsbane," a voice said from behind us. We turned around and saw Arlene Braxton. Arlene was Jonathan's mother. I hadn't noticed her when we first walked out and was surprised when she spoke up. She hobbled over with her cane, a large, wide-brimmed straw hat on her head. Her dress was a bright purple floral that came almost to her ankles. "Do you know what Wolfsbane is?" she asked.

I glanced at Lucy and shook my head. "No, I don't think I do. The name is familiar, but I can't quite place it."

She leaned on her cane and turned to the plant. "Wolfsbane, also known as monkshood and aconite. It's a beautiful flowering plant, but it is also one of the most poisonous plants around." She turned back to look at us with one eyebrow raised. "It's best not to fool with it."

I was surprised to find out Penny had a poisonous plant right here on the edge of her patio. "Really?"

She nodded. "Oh, sure. Lots of people in medieval times used it to poison their enemies. Isn't that right, Elise?"

We turned as Elise Donovan stepped onto the patio from a paved pathway coming from the garden. She tilted her head beneath a decorated white straw hat. "You've got to love those medieval people, don't you? If you've got a problem with somebody, you just poison them." She shrugged.

I nodded. "I guess so."

"Have you been to the garden party before?" Arlene asked us.

"No, we've never been here before," Lucy said. "It

sure is beautiful here on the patio. I bet Penny's garden is absolutely stunning."

Arlene, still leaning on her cane, nodded. "Yes, it is a stunning garden. She takes the credit for making it so beautiful, but you know she hires people to come and take care of it. It's not like that woman is ever going to get her fingers dirty." She made a face.

I was taken aback that she spoke openly that way about her daughter-in-law. "It would be an awful lot of work for one person to take care of," I pointed out.

She nodded. "That's true, but you would think that she could do something since she's calling it *her* garden. I mean, she didn't even pay for it. Jonathan pays for it. But what are you going to do? Some people are just that way."

I wasn't sure what to say to that, so I glanced back at the table with the boxes of desserts. "I guess we had better take the desserts out of the boxes." I stepped back over to the table and opened up a box.

"So that's Wolfsbane?" Lucy asked, nodding at the plant. "How did the medieval people use it to kill someone?"

Arlene shrugged. "Oh, I don't know. I guess they put it in somebody's food or in their tea or something of that nature. Back then, people didn't know much about anything, so I suppose they might not have even questioned if it tasted a little funny."

"Probably not," I said, removing the cake and setting it on the cake stand that Penny had provided. The cake stand was crystal, and it made the cake look absolutely stunning. "There now. That cake stand is befitting a beautiful cake." The cake was frosted in chocolate buttercream, and I had added small candy flowers in pink, yellow, and white to it.

"That is a lovely cake," Arlene agreed. "I'm going to get me a big slice of that."

"It looks delicious," Elise agreed.

"Isn't that a lovely cake?" someone said from behind us. We turned to see Rebecca Adams had stepped out onto the patio. Rebecca was a friend of Penny's, and she was dressed in a pink silk dress and an enormous pink hat. I was beginning to feel out of place with no hat.

"I wouldn't miss having a slice of that cake for the world, if I were you, ladies," Lucy said. "It's the pièce de résistance of all the desserts."

Rebecca smirked and turned to Arlene. "Educating the ladies on medieval poisons, Arlene?"

The French doors opened before she could answer, and Penny stepped outside. "Oh. Are you two still here?"

I smiled, even though she was frowning at us. "Oh, yes, we were just unpacking the desserts. We won't be long."

Elise turned and scowled at Penny, but she didn't seem to notice.

Penny sighed. "My guests will arrive any time now. I need you to hurry up and set everything out for me, please. And then you can go."

My heart sank just a little. I really wanted to see that garden. "Of course," I said. "We sure love the flowers that you've got here around your patio."

"I bet your garden is stunning," Lucy hinted.

She nodded and turned around, heading back toward the French doors. "Yes, it certainly is. Thank you for your services, Allie." She turned to Rebecca. "You're not going to just stand there all day, are you? It seems like you could do something to help."

"Of course." Rebecca followed her back inside the house without a glance behind her.

Arlene made a clucking sound with her tongue. "Now you see Penny's true colors. But I, for one, appreciate you two providing the desserts. I know they're going to be spectacular."

I nodded and smiled at Arlene. "You're welcome. You'll have to let me know how you enjoyed them."

Lucy and I got to work setting out the desserts.

CHAPTER 4

"You know it's not right, Penny!"

Lucy and I turned to see who had spoken. Elise was standing close to Penny, her cheeks red.

Penny smiled smugly. "I was just trying to be accommodating. Can you blame me? You know everybody expects so much out of me. You can get away with doing next to nothing, but not me."

Elise sputtered. "What? What are you talking about? You're just making excuses now."

Lucy and I glanced at one another. We were just about finished setting the desserts out and Elise and Penny were standing just inside of the French doors.

"Don't get so excited, Elise," Penny purred, grinning.

"Penny, I swear, one of these days you're going to get what's coming to you."

Penny laughed and went back into another room.

"I wonder what that's about?" Lucy whispered.

"Lucy! Allie! It's so good to see you here," Dori Kellogg said as she floated past Elise and through the French doors. She was wearing a straw hat, which apparently was a necessity for a garden party I was learning, and a cute pale blue blouse and skirt set. Dori Kellogg had a son and daughter the same age as my kids, and we had been involved in the PTA together.

Lucy and I smiled. "Hi Dori, haven't seen you in forever," I said.

She smiled and came over to hug me, then looked at the dessert table. "It's been ages, hasn't it? We really need to get together and do something fun. How are you, Lucy?" She put her hand on Lucy's arm and gave it a squeeze. Dori was the demonstrative type.

I set some tartlets on the table. "I'm doing great, Dori. It's good to see you again. It has been forever."

She turned to me. "Allie, don't tell me you made all these delectable desserts?"

"Yes, and Lucy helped me when Penny asked me to make the desserts for her party."

"It was a lot of fun," Lucy said, meeting my eyes. If we didn't get out of here soon, Penny was going to come and throw us out. I could hear more guests arriving and excited chatter coming from inside the house, and I longed to hang around for a while and see what happened at these garden parties.

"I'm so glad Penny asked you to make the desserts. She's been getting them from a patisserie over in Bangor, and between the three of us, they leave something to be desired, if you know what I mean." She gave me a knowing look, and I smiled. "Penny is so cheap. I hope she paid you well."

I hesitated, then decided to ignore the remark. "Well, I certainly hope everybody's going to be happy with everything that I made. I think my favorite is the layer cake, but you'll have to try them all and let me know what you think." I folded up the empty bakery box.

"You can bet I'm going to try them all. You know me. I'm not one to pass up anything sweet." She chuckled as more guests flowed out onto the patio from inside the house. I glanced over at the open door. Penny was nowhere to be seen.

"We probably should go," I reluctantly said to Lucy.

She nodded. "I guess so."

"Oh, what's your rush?" Dori asked. "It'll be such fun to catch up, won't it? Hang around a while."

I smiled, glancing back at the open French doors. I

didn't want to get into trouble with Penny, but I also didn't want to seem rude and take off when Dori wanted to visit. Besides, there was that garden that I really wanted to get a good look at. I needed more ideas for my garden, and I just knew that Penny's garden would give me all sorts of ideas.

We stood and chatted with Dori for a while as more people stepped out onto the patio. There were round tables with white tablecloths, and fresh flower arrangements in the centers set out in the yard. I didn't know how much this cost Penny to put together, but I was pretty sure it was a pretty penny.

A woman in a beige uniform came out, carrying a silver tea tray with a pink floral teapot and delicate China cups on it. Penny really was serious about her tea. The woman put the tray on a nearby table as another maid exited the house with another tea tray. This one had a white teapot with yellow flowers on it. She set it next to the first one and headed back into the house.

"I could use a cup of tea," Lucy said, eyeing the two teapots.

I wanted to nudge her and tell her no, but Dori was standing right there. Lucy slipped over to the table and poured herself a cup.

"We really need to see one another more often," Dori said to me. I turned back to look at her, my mind struggling to focus on what she had just said—Lucy was going to get us into trouble.

I smiled and nodded. "Yes, that's right."

Just then, Penny stepped out onto the patio, holding a cup of tea. My heart sank. It would only be a moment or two before she realized that both Lucy and I were still here. Would she demand that we leave? No. She wasn't a woman who would make a scene, especially not at her own garden party, but I felt bad for still hanging around. She had hired us to make her desserts, not hang out and be guests.

"This is tasty," Lucy said, holding up her teacup to me. "I don't know how they make their tea here, but it's really good. Not at all bitter."

"Oh, I love a good cup of tea," Dori said. "Allie, let's go get a cup of tea."

I shot Lucy a look as I followed Dori over to the tea trays as two more trays with teapots were brought out. I just knew that we were going to get into trouble for this. Dori poured herself a cup of tea, and I did the same. It was green tea, and I added a bit of sugar and took a sip. Lucy was right. This was the best green tea I'd ever tasted, even though I usually didn't care for green tea.

"Ladies," Penny said, calling everyone to attention. "We've got so much to discuss today. You all know that I want to make some changes to the gardening society, and today is the perfect day to think about those changes."

Rebecca stood next to her and nodded. "I agree. Changes are in order."

There were nods of agreement as people began pouring themselves cups of tea. "But I have a sumptuous luncheon planned, and then we will take a look at my beautiful garden," Penny continued. "I am so excited about the new varieties of flowers that I planted this year, and I think you'll all agree that this is absolutely the most perfect garden ever."

I heard a soft snort behind me. "Like she planted anything."

I didn't dare look over my shoulder to see who had said it, but I couldn't help but smile. I took another sip of my tea, wondering if I could get the name of the brand so I could get some for home.

Penny took a sip of tea from the cup in her hand and swayed just a bit. "I hope you all enjoy yourselves. I even hired Allie McSwain to make the desserts."

At that moment, our eyes locked, and she narrowed them at me. I didn't want to correct her for using my former married name. I was, after all, an uninvited guest, so I just smiled at her.

She took another sip of her tea without looking away. Great. Lucy and I were going to be in trouble.

Thankfully, I had gotten the money upfront for the desserts I had made.

Penny swayed again, and she reached out and steadied herself by holding onto a nearby table. That was odd. Had she been drinking? That wasn't very ladylike when she was hosting a garden party.

She took another sip of her tea and set the cup down. I suddenly realized Penny was breathing hard as if she had been exercising, but I couldn't imagine she had done enough inside the house to be out of breath. She picked up the cup again to take another sip as everybody stood around expectantly, waiting for her to continue what she was saying, when she suddenly crashed to the ground, the teacup slamming against the concrete and breaking into a hundred pieces. There were screams from her guests.

For a moment, everybody stood frozen, me included. Then I hurried over to Penny's side and knelt. "Penny? Are you okay? What's going on?" I looked over my shoulder at Lucy, who was heading in my direction. "Call an ambulance."

I turned back to Penny. Her eyes were wide open, and she seemed to be gagging, and having a hard time breathing. I gave her a shake. "Penny? What's going on? Are you all right?" I could feel everyone gathering closer to us, and I turned to look over my shoulder again. "What's going on with her? Does she have seizures? Or any allergies?" I remembered the walnut allergy, but I hadn't made anything with walnuts.

People shook their heads, uncertain of what to do. I reached out and put my hand on her wrist to check her pulse while Lucy made the phone call. It took me at least twenty seconds before I felt the pulse in her wrist, and it felt weak. "Penny, stay with me." Penny just stared blankly at me as her breathing grew more labored.

I glanced back over my shoulder, searching for Arlene. She was family, and she would know if Penny had some sort of medical condition. Where was Jonathan?

I spotted Arlene standing back, leaning against one of the decorated patio poles. She watched what was unfolding intently but had made no move to come closer as the other ladies had done. "Arlene, do you know if Penny has any medical conditions? Is there any medication we can give her?"

Arlene leaned on her cane and didn't answer immediately. Finally, she gave a quick shake of her head. "No, I'm not aware of any medical conditions or medications that she might be on. We'll have to wait for the ambulance to get here."

I turned back to Penny, who was turning blue, and prayed that the ambulance would arrive soon.

CHAPTER 5

We watched as the EMTs carted Penny off on a gurney through the side gate. Her guests stood around, murmuring to one another in small groups. Lucy and I turned to look at each other.

"Well, that was unexpected. I hope she's going to be okay," Lucy whispered.

I nodded. "I sure hope so."

Dori scooted over to where we stood on the edge of the patio. "Well, girls, who would have seen that coming?" She shook her head and glanced at the open gate. "What a shame. This is probably the biggest day of the year for Penny."

I crossed my arms in front of me. "Penny looked forward to her garden party. Hopefully she'll be okay." I had a bad feeling about this, though. Between Penny's labored breathing and the pallor of her skin, I wasn't sure it was going to turn out well for her.

Dori shrugged. "Well, you never can tell. Maybe there will be a new Mrs. Braxton having her own garden party here next year."

Lucy and I both whipped our heads around to look at her. There was a smile on her face, and that made me wonder if she knew something she wasn't saying.

"What?" Lucy asked.

Dori shook her head. "Oh, nothing. You know me. I always have to be the crass one. At least that's what Penny says." She chuckled. "Well, I guess there's not much point in us hanging around. I bet they aren't going to serve lunch now that our hostess is gone."

"I've lost my appetite," I said.

She glanced back at the dessert table. "Well, I haven't. I didn't eat anything today because I was anticipating the luncheon. I'm going to grab some of those tartlets you made." With that, she turned and hurried over to the table.

Lucy and I looked at one another. "I guess Dori's not tiptoeing around anything," Lucy said.

I nodded. "She sure isn't." I didn't know what Dori and Penny's relationship was really like, but from the few comments Dori had made, I was getting a picture of it.

I heard a tapping behind me, and then someone said, "I guess you never can tell what life is going to bring you."

We turned around to see Arlene standing there, leaning on her cane.

"No, I guess you can't," I said. "Penny never mentioned that she had any health issues?" It seemed like with Arlene being her mother-in-law, she would have mentioned it to her at least once if she had some ongoing health problems.

She shook her head. "Nope. She never said a word to me. But that's Penny for you. She mostly keeps things to herself. Complains to all the world, but doesn't say a word to me."

Arlene was smiling as she spoke, which made me wonder. "She probably just doesn't want to worry you."

Arlene laughed. "Yeah, that must be it. No, that isn't it. Penny is just an awful person. She's been a problem ever since she married my son." She turned and looked back at the house.

"Where is Jonathan? He was here before the party started," I said.

She turned back to me. "He went golfing. He left just as everyone began arriving."

I nodded. "Did you call him?"

Her brow furrowed. "Whatever for?"

I frowned. "Because his wife was just taken to the hospital." Why would she ask such a question?

She shrugged and jerked her head toward Rebecca, who was sobbing and dabbing at her eyes with a napkin. "That one will tell him." She turned and hobbled back toward the house.

Lucy and I looked at each other. "It's probably time that we left," she said.

I nodded, then turned and looked back in the garden's direction. I meant to leave. I really did. "Well, with everything going on, I think now is the perfect time for us to get a look at that garden."

Lucy's eyes widened. "Let's go."

* * *

Penny's garden had been just as beautiful as we had imagined it to be. There were stone fountains along with stone figures scattered throughout the entire garden. Angels and woodland animals were tucked into every crevice. The paths were done in red brick with stones set in concrete to outline the bricks. She must have had every variety of flower and bush that grew native to Maine as well as a few that didn't. As you can imagine, a garden that spans more than a quarter of an acre was expansive, and we had taken our time walking through it, figuring there was nobody to run us off. And believe me, there were no gnomes in that garden.

I had made a nice roasted chicken for dinner, but then Alec texted me that he would be late, so I was sitting in the living room with Dixie in my lap and a good book. It was just after nine o'clock when I heard Alec's key in the door.

In a few moments, he entered the living room. "Hey. I hope you didn't wait dinner on me."

"Of course I did. What kept you?" I closed my book, set Dixie on the ground, and went to him, kissing him. "Anything exciting?"

His brow furrowed. "Tell me again who you made those desserts for?"

I frowned. "Penny Braxton. Why?"

His eyes widened. "Because she died."

I gasped. "What? What do you mean, she died? How do you know?"

"The ER doctor called me, saying that it looked like she died under suspicious circumstances. Poisoning, to be exact."

My mouth dropped open. "Are you serious? That's why she was having breathing problems, right? Oh my gosh. Wait until I call Lucy. She will never believe it." I turned to grab my phone from the end table.

"Don't call her just yet. I've barely finished telling her husband and mother-in-law that she died, and no one else knows about it. Let's give them the night to process it. I'm starving. What's for dinner?"

"I roasted a chicken. Let's eat." I hurried to the kitchen and laid my phone down on the kitchen counter. I would call Lucy as soon as I had all the details. "Why did the doctor suspect poisoning?"

"Because it looks like she was asphyxiated, although he won't know for sure until the autopsy is done. But there were enough red flags that he thought he should report it." He went to the refrigerator, got the sweet tea out, and then got two glasses from the cupboard.

"Asphyxiation? I thought you said she was poisoned?" I opened the oven and took the chicken out. I had put the lid on the baking dish to keep it from drying out while I waited for him to come home.

He nodded as he put ice into the glasses. "There was redness in her mouth and throat, and her breathing was cut off. Nothing they tried could get her airway to reopen. At first, they thought it was an asthma attack, but nothing worked, and the redness told him it was something else."

I set the roasting pan on the table. "Wow. It was so odd. It seemed like she was fine when we first got there. She complained that she had allergies, which she was upset about because, of course, because she was having a garden party."

"It must be tough having a great big garden that you're allergic to." He poured sweet tea over the ice, and it cracked.

I nodded as I got the baked potatoes out of the oven and put them on a plate, then brought the salad to the table, thinking this over. "She also said she was allergic to walnuts, but I didn't use any walnuts in anything I made. And besides that, she only ate one of my key lime tartlets, nothing else."

He looked at me, one eyebrow raised. "Don't tell me I'm going to have to investigate you for poisoning a woman with walnuts."

I waved away the thought. "I would not have expected her to be poisoned. However, some people were behaving rather strangely. Like her mother-in-law. She didn't seem particularly upset that her daughter-in-law was having a problem with her health, and neither did Dori Kellogg. Dori and Penny go way back, but I've always had the feeling that the two didn't care for one another much." The last thing I would have expected was for Penny to have died at her own garden party. But even less expected was that somebody would have murdered her.

"Dori Kellogg? I don't think I know her."

"She has kids Thad and Jennifer's age. Did her husband say who he thought might want to kill her?"

He shook his head. "No, he was as distraught as you can imagine, but he didn't offer any insight into what might have happened."

Then I remembered something Arlene had said to Lucy and me. I turned to him. "Wolfsbane."

He looked at me, one eyebrow cocked. "What?"

"Wolfsbane. It's this plant with these gorgeous purple flowers. Arlene Braxton told us it was highly poisonous and that people in the medieval centuries would poison their enemies with it. Penny had this big flowerpot of it sitting right on the edge of the patio. Can you imagine? Why would you plant a poisonous plant and then have it right there on your patio? It didn't make sense to me when she told us about it."

His brow furrowed. "She had it growing right there on her patio? It really doesn't make a lot of sense, does it?"

I shook my head. "No, it doesn't. I bet that's what killed her. Oh. And Penny was drinking from a cup of tea when she came out to speak to her guests. It fell and broke when she collapsed."

"I didn't see a broken teacup when I investigated the property."

I turned to him. "That means the killer was there.

They picked up that teacup and cleaned up the mess so you wouldn't know what killed her. I swear, it has to be the Wolfsbane that was used to poison her."

He nodded. "I'll go back to the house and take a sample of it tomorrow. It will take some time to get the toxicology report." He sat down as I put the plates on the table.

"Lucy and I have some work to do."

He chuckled and carved the chicken. Alec was the lead detective in our small town, but Lucy and I had worked on many murder investigations, and we frequently came up with information that was helpful to a case. We were going to sort this out.

CHAPTER 6

I removed the lid from my coffee cup and inhaled deeply. Nothing beats the smell of freshly brewed coffee.

Mr. Winters looked at me over the top of his glasses. "Red, it's not going to do you any good if you don't actually put it in your mouth and swallow," he informed me.

I opened my eyes to look at him. "That's not true. There was a study that said just the smell of freshly brewed coffee can give you the same pick-me-up that drinking it does."

Lucy shook her head. "I'm not going to fall for that one. I'm going to drink every drop of my latte." She took a sip of hers and grinned. "See? It made me smile. Inhaling the scent of coffee could never do that for you."

I chuckled, and replaced the lid on my cup of caramel latte and took a sip. "You're right, it is a lot better to drink it, isn't it? I need some caffeine running through my veins, or I'm never going to stay awake today." We normally began our day with a run, but I couldn't get myself up and moving this morning, and after giving it my best shot for a while, I gave up. It was because I had lain awake most of the night, thinking about what had happened to Penny Braxton. She had died right in front of our eyes. Or at least, she was well on her way to being dead right in front of our eyes. She did the actual dying at the hospital. But why hadn't we seen the killer slip her the poison? We hadn't even known anything was going on.

Mr. Winters leaned forward. "Okay, what do you know about Penny Braxton? Spill it."

I sighed and shook my head. "Not nearly enough. What have you heard?"

He frowned, his forehead wrinkling with the effort. "No, don't you do that. I know what you're trying to do; you're trying to find out what I know without telling me what you know. I'm not going to fall for it. Spill it."

"Honestly, Mr. Winters," Lucy said, taking another sip of her coffee. "Allie and I were at the garden party, and we saw her collapse, but we didn't see who poisoned her."

I nodded. "That's right. We were right there, and we didn't see anything suspicious."

His eyes widened. "What? How did you get an invitation to that garden party? Penny Braxton only invited the crème de la crème, Sandy Harbor's elite. Not that I'm trying to cast aspersions upon either of you, but I didn't know you ran with that crowd."

Lucy and I both laughed. "Oh, believe me, we don't run with that crowd," I said, shaking my head and smiling. "Penny asked me to make some desserts. Don't you remember?"

His eyes widened. "Ah, you're right. I forgot all about that. Okay, so you were there at the party setting out your tasty wares, and somebody slipped her some poison. Well, who did it? Who was at the party? And who hated her enough to kill her?"

I nodded. "That's the question of the day. I knew most of the people who were there, and I really couldn't tell you who might have wanted to kill her. At least, I couldn't tell you just yet. But Lucy and I will find out. You can bet on it."

Lucy turned to me. "We make quite a team, don't we? We should call ourselves the sleuthing gals. We'll find the killer, Mr. Winters. Just you wait and see."

I nodded. "We certainly will. Now, Mr. Winters, what do you know?"

He shook his head. "That's just it. I don't know anything. You know me; I've never run around with the hoity-toity set. They wouldn't have allowed me anywhere near that party. At least the two of you got inside so you could take a look around. Was anybody acting peculiar? Was anybody angry or upset?"

I thought about it for a moment. "I wish I had an answer for you, but I really don't." Arlene Braxton, Penny's mother-in-law, hadn't even tried to pretend that she liked her daughter-in-law. But she's an elderly woman. Was she really capable of murder? I wasn't sure, but I didn't think so, in spite of her knowledge of Wolfsbane.

Mr. Winters took a sip of his black coffee. "I expect the two of you to report back to me when you find out something important. We have to figure out who killed Penny Braxton. I didn't care for the woman, not that I knew her well, of course, but we still need to figure out who her killer was."

I nodded absently as one of the coffee shop employees came to clear the table next to ours. Whoever had sat there had left empty coffee cups, as well as napkins, paper plates, and the small bags that baked goods usually came in. My mother would have been ashamed of me if I had left a table at an eating establishment in such a shape. The woman had long blonde hair tied back in a ponytail and frowned as she gathered up the trash.

"Sometimes people don't think, do they?" I said to her.

She turned and looked at me, eyes widening. "Yeah, sometimes I'm shocked at how people behave in here. I would never have gotten away with leaving this kind of trash on the table when I was a kid—and these were all adults." She chuckled lightly. "But I guess that's what I get paid for, right?"

"Yes, but you don't need people to make it harder for you," Lucy said.

She smiled and nodded, picking up another coffee cup. "You know, I don't mean to eavesdrop, but I heard you were talking about Penny Braxton." She hesitated, and I felt bad that we had been speaking loudly enough for anybody to overhear us.

I nodded. "Yes, it's a terrible shame that she was murdered." I hoped she wasn't related to her. I would have been completely embarrassed if she was, and we had been caught talking about her murder.

She made a face. "I hate to speak ill of the dead, but she wasn't the nicest person. She would come in here sometimes, order us around, and treat us as if we were her servants or something. I guess I shouldn't complain because, like I said, I get paid to do this job, right? But it was just the way she did it. As if she owned the place and didn't have to show any kind of respect toward us." She made a face again. "But if you ask me, I think her best friend, Rebecca, is the one who killed her. It's all anyone is talking about."

I was surprised to hear her say this about Rebecca. She and Penny seemed to get along very well. "Oh? Why do you say that?"

She gathered up the paper plates and used a clean napkin from the dispenser to gather up the dirty napkins, setting them on top of the plates. "Because they were rich folks. They were mean and hateful, not just to people they thought were beneath them, but toward each other, too. I've seen Rebecca come in here plenty of times with her rich friends, and they would all talk down about Penny and laugh. They apparently thought they were better than she was." She rolled her eyes and grinned. "I guess even rich folk have their problems. They talk about each other just as badly as anybody else does. Maybe more so. People they think are their friends may not be."

I smiled. "Did they say anything specific about Penny?"

She thought about it for a moment. "Well, they said that one of these days, Penny was going to get what was coming to her. I don't know what that was in reference to because I just happened to walk up on them in the middle of a conversation. But they acted as if they didn't see me, and didn't stop talking. Apparently, Penny thought she was better than they were, and didn't have any problems letting them know. She ordered them around, and she thought her garden was better than theirs. Can you believe it? They were sitting around talking about gardens." She rolled her eyes again. "I guess when you've got so much money that you don't have to worry about paying the bills, you have time to sit around and argue about who has the nicest flower garden. I can't imagine being concerned about something like that, but I guess it's a big thing to all of them."

Lucy nodded. "Yes, it seems like in the late spring, early summer, that flower garden is all-important to a certain group of people."

"You mean rich people," she corrected. "I don't know what they get out of it. I guess it must be bragging rights." She whipped out a wet cloth and began wiping the table down.

"I guess like you said, when you don't have to worry about paying the bills, you free up your time to worry about other things," I said, pondering what she said about Rebecca. I would have sworn that she and Penny were best friends and didn't have any trouble between them, but now I wondered.

The woman straightened up and picked up the

trash from the table. "Well, I didn't mean to interrupt you folks. But one thing I have learned is that rich folks can be evil, and they will stop at nothing to get whatever they want. You all have a good day." She turned and headed to a nearby trashcan. When she was out of earshot, I turned to Mr. Winters and Lucy.

"That's interesting."

Mr. Winters nodded and took a sip of his coffee. "Rich folks are different, that's for sure, but I wouldn't say they're all evil. Unless, of course, they are, in which case we'll call them evil." He winked at me.

We needed to have a talk with Rebecca.

CHAPTER 7

We sat and visited with Mr. Winters for nearly an hour, and then I finally decided that I had better get going. I had a few errands to run and a week and a half's worth of laundry that wasn't going to do itself.

As Lucy and I stepped outside the coffee shop, I spotted Rebecca near my car. She had a handkerchief that she was dabbing at her eyes with, and when she saw us, she cried out, "Allie! Lucy!"

Lucy and I glanced at one another and then turned back to Rebecca as she waved at us with the handkerchief. We crossed the parking lot to her. *What on earth was she doing hanging around my car?*

"Good morning, Rebecca," I said with a nod when

we got closer. "How are you doing today? You've been on my mind."

"Yes, I've been thinking about you too, Rebecca," Lucy added. "We're so sorry about Penny."

When we got closer, I could see the smeared mascara beneath her eyes. She sobbed loudly, "Oh, I just can't believe that Penny is gone. Dead. I haven't slept a wink since the party. I just can't get her off my mind."

I nodded sympathetically. The poor thing *looked* like she hadn't slept a wink. "I'm so sorry. I know this must be so hard for you."

She sniffed and nodded. "Yes, Penny and I were close. Closer than sisters. We knew each other practically all our lives, and we did so much together. I keep asking myself who would want to kill her. Has your husband come up with any suspects?"

I shook my head. "No, but it's early in the investigation. Sometimes these things take more time than we would like for them to be solved."

She nodded and dabbed at her eyes again. "I can understand that, I guess. But all I want is to look the killer in the eye and ask them why. Why would they kill somebody who was as sweet and wonderful as Penny?"

I wondered if she really believed Penny was as sweet and wonderful as she was saying, because, according to the employee at the coffee shop, she didn't think so. "I know it seems like knowing the answer to that question might help, but it probably won't. I mean, Penny is still gone, right?" I hated for her to get her hopes up that having answers, like the reason for her murder, might help, but it probably wouldn't. It certainly wouldn't change anything.

She nodded, and tears filled her eyes again. "I know. I know it doesn't change a thing, but I still would like to know why. And I certainly want to know who. Whoever it is deserves to suffer. I wish we still had the death penalty here in Maine. I don't know why they did away with it."

"I'm so sorry," Lucy said sympathetically.

She dabbed at her eyes with the handkerchief again. Few people still carried cloth handkerchiefs, but that was what she was using. "Just let me get my hands on that person. I'll make them sorry they did what they did."

"Rebecca, do you have any idea who might have wanted to kill Penny?" I asked, hoping to steer her attention away from hurting somebody.

She took a deep breath. "I've been thinking about this. What else do I have to do, right? I'm certainly not sleeping. And the only person who I think could be evil enough to kill Penny would be her mother-in-law. Arlene." She looked at me and then at Lucy. "That old woman is just evil. She's always treated Penny terribly, and it wouldn't surprise me a bit if she killed her."

"Really?" I asked, and then I remembered again our brief conversation about Wolfsbane and the beautiful purple plant that was on Penny's patio, and my heart beat faster. Could it have been Arlene?

She nodded. "Yes, when Penny and Jonathan first got married, Penny was sure that his mother would be the end of their marriage. That woman would come over to her house all the time and complain about everything she did. It seemed that the house was never clean enough, the kids weren't being raised right, and she wasn't a good enough wife to her son. That was back before they had money to hire someone to do the housework." She chuckled. "Penny used to say that as soon as she had enough money, she would hire a housekeeper and a nanny to take care of everything so that her mother-in-law couldn't complain about her. And when Jonathan did make money in the stock market, that's exactly what she did. She hired as much help as she could afford, and that took away a lot of the complaints from Arlene."

Lucy shook her head. "Wouldn't that be a lot of fun? Hiring people to take care of all the stuff you don't want to deal with?"

Rebecca nodded. "Oh, yes, you know it would be.

Penny always said it was unfortunate that the kids were already out of diapers by the time she was able to hire a nanny. She would have liked to have missed out on all of that." She laughed. "That was Penny. She hated to get her hands dirty."

"What about her garden?" I asked. "Did she get her hands dirty in her garden?" I already knew the answer to this, but I wanted to see what she would say.

She laughed again. "Are you kidding? Penny had an entire team of gardeners to take care of all the dirty work. All she did was point out what was wrong with it or decide on what flowers and plants to put in there. It was an award-winning garden, to be sure, and something to be envied, but she didn't do any of the hard work herself."

"It was one of the most beautiful gardens I've ever seen," Lucy said. "I would love to have a garden like that. I would spend all my time outdoors if I had one like it."

I nodded. "Me too. It's absolutely beautiful." I didn't have the money, the energy, or the time to create a garden like Penny's, but I had gotten some ideas about what to do with my garden to make it a little nicer when I took a quick tour of hers.

She smiled. "Yes, as I said, it is an award-winning garden. Penny was always so proud of it. I tell you, when the garden society toured it, they were in awe. I have a nice garden too, but I have to admit that mine isn't nearly as nice as hers. Who's got that kind of money to spend on a garden?" She shrugged. "Well, at least she spent most of her time doing what she enjoyed, and we can all hope to do that in our own lives, can't we?"

I nodded. "Yes, it's good to live a life where you do the things that you truly enjoy."

She sighed. "I just don't know what I'm going to do with myself without her. I told my husband that I feel so lost now." Tears welled up in her eyes again.

"Rebecca, do you really think that Arlene could have killed Penny?" I asked. Arlene seemed like a pleasant woman, but she had to have been in her late eighties. It seemed like by that age, she would have settled down and not been thinking about how to murder her daughter-in-law.

She nodded and stepped in closer. "I do. That woman was fixated on Penny. She just couldn't stand her. She asked her son to divorce Penny and find another woman who would take care of him the way he deserved to be taken care of." She rolled her eyes. "If you ask me, that woman is obsessed with her son. She only had the one, you know, and I guess she devoted all her time to him when he was younger and didn't know how to stop once he got older and was married. But do I think she could have killed her? Yes. I really do. I hope your husband is going to talk to her. I think he will find out some interesting things about her if he does."

I nodded. "Sometimes family squabbles can go on for a very long time and can get very serious."

"Exactly. Please tell him to speak very carefully to her and to listen to what she says because I think he'll realize when he does that, he'll find that she is Penny's killer."

"I'll certainly mention it to him," I said. Alec would make up his own mind about who he wanted to talk to and what he believed about what they had to say. I hated to think that Arlene might be Penny's killer, though. It didn't seem right that she might have to spend her final years behind bars.

"Well, if you'll excuse me, I had better get into the coffee shop. I need something to help me stay alert. If I don't get some sleep soon, I might self-destruct." She chuckled. "It's been good talking to you ladies."

"It's good seeing you, too," I said. "If you need a shoulder to cry on, we are here for you."

She smiled. "That is so sweet of you, Allie. I will definitely keep that in mind. See you later."

We watched her head to the coffee shop, and when she was inside, Lucy turned to look at me. "That's interesting."

I nodded. "It certainly is. I hate to think of Arlene as a killer, but we have to look into it. A family squabble that has gotten out of control may have been the end of Penny Braxton. And if that's so, we are going to get to the bottom of it."

CHAPTER 8

"How did I get to marry the most handsome man in the world?" I gazed at Alec over an intimate table at the local Bradbury Café. We had just placed our orders, and we were waiting for what I was sure would be a delectable lunch. I was inhaling the scent of freshly baked sourdough roll while we waited.

He shrugged. "Luck, I guess."

I chuckled and rolled my eyes. "Oh yeah, I'm sure it was just luck. Okay, spill it. What's going on with the investigation?" I split my roll in half and opened a little container of butter.

"We went through the house and gathered stuff. I don't know yet if any of it is going to yield anything, of course, but I'm hopeful."

I nodded. "And the lab reports?"

"The lab reports say that she was poisoned with aconite."

I looked at him. "Aconite? What is that?"

"Wolfsbane." One eyebrow rose, and he picked up his glass of iced tea.

I nodded. "Of course. She had that beautiful plant near her patio. I just can't imagine why anybody would keep a poisonous plant right on their patio. Anyone could get a hold of that." I shook my head. "Some people don't think."

"Agreed. Even if Penny knew what it was, and she informed her guests, I could still see somebody accidentally handling it and possibly poisoning themselves. Especially if there were children about."

I glanced at him. I knew he was thinking about our granddaughter, Lilly. She was fifteen months old now and constantly on the move. We had to keep an eye on her at all times, even though we had childproofed our home. "It doesn't make sense, does it?"

He shook his head, set his glass down, and grabbed a butter knife to butter his roll. "It's foolish if you ask me."

"What else did you find? What pieces of evidence did you take back to the station?"

He gazed at me. "The teapots, some cups, and some clothing. But I'm sure that by the time we realized she had been poisoned, the teapot and cups had been washed, so there's probably nothing in them. In fact, I'm sure everything was cleaned up rather well," he sighed.

"That's disappointing," I said. "The killer must have known that, too. It was going to take the medical examiner time to figure out what she died from, and that time gave them an open door to clean everything up." I looked up as the waitress brought our food. I was having the clam chowder, and Alec had ordered a hearty beef stew. The café only had a few dishes on the menu, but they were unbeatable, and they did a brisk business.

"I'm starving," he said. "I talked to her husband again." He looked at me.

"And?"

"He has no idea who would have killed her."

Shaking my head, I took a bite of my clam chowder. "This is fabulous. There's nothing like a good bowl of clam chowder." Living so close to the beach meant a wonderful selection of fresh seafood in almost every restaurant, and I never tired of it.

"I probably should have gotten clam chowder," he said, taking a bite of his stew.

"The stew isn't good?" I looked up at him.

He shook his head. "No, it's great. The clam chowder just looks amazing."

"It is amazing. What did Jonathan have to say?"

He gazed at me. "I heard a little rumor about him, and that's why I went to talk to him again—that he was seeing someone on the side."

I gasped. "What? Are you kidding me? I can't imagine Jonathan Braxton cheating on his wife. Did you ask him about it?"

He nodded. "And he denied it. I don't even have the name of a woman, so it's not like I can ask her."

I frowned. "Who told you he was seeing someone? Why didn't they know who he was seeing?"

"Rebecca Adams told me about her. She said she didn't know who the woman was because she saw her from behind when she went to a restaurant in Bangor. Jonathan denied it and said that it was probably when he was out with Penny. Rebecca, of course, would have known if it was Penny. Jonathan does genuinely seem upset about the death of his wife, so I hesitate to push that angle without having a name or more evidence that it's even happening."

I nodded and tore off a piece of my roll, then dipped it in my clam chowder. "Without a name, there isn't much you can do. I just can't see him cheating on Penny, though." I knew Jonathan well enough to know that he was a good guy, and cheating seemed out of the realm of possibilities for him. I could be wrong about it, but it just didn't seem like something he would do.

I glanced up as Julia Desmond approached our table. Julia owned the café, and I had known her for years. I smiled. "Hi Julia, how are you?"

She smiled and gave me a nod, then looked at Alec. "I'm doing great, Allie. Alec, I heard you were working on an investigation into a murder." It wasn't a question; it was a statement. News traveled quickly in this town.

Alec nodded. "Yes, I'm looking into Penny Braxton's murder."

Julia's cheeks were pink, and she inhaled. "Penny was a friend of mine. I still can't get over the fact that she's gone."

"I'm sorry to hear that," Alec said. "Please accept our condolences."

"Yes, I'm so sorry, Julia. It's come as a shock to everyone, I think," I said.

She gave me a weak smile. Julia was in her sixties, and she wore her blonde hair short, cropped close to her head. "Thank you. I appreciate hearing that. I've known Penny for years. Decades. We met right after she graduated from high school. She worked for me at another little restaurant I had at the edge of town. She was one of my best waitresses, and we became friends."

"I didn't know you owned another restaurant." I picked up my glass of tea to take a sip.

She nodded. "Yes, I opened it years ago, back when I was still wet behind the ears." She chuckled. "I was far too young to be running my own business back then, but I didn't know it until it was too late. I lost everything and had to shut it down. But it was a great learning experience for me. Plus, I got to be friends with a lot of people, including Penny. So, you can imagine, after having known her for all those years, how it breaks my heart that she was murdered." She turned to Alec. "Alec, do you have any idea who killed her?"

Alec shook his head. "I'm afraid not. But I'm working on it, and I'm hoping to have some answers soon."

She nodded. "Good. I just want her killer put behind bars. But do you mind if I fill you in on a little something that might be of help?"

Alec leaned forward. "Of course. Go ahead."

She nodded. "Because I was close to Penny, I know her husband well, too. And between the three of us, I never really liked him. He thinks too highly of himself. There's just always been something about him I never liked." I was surprised to hear her talk this way about Jonathan. I always thought he was a pleasant person, and I wondered what made her dislike him.

"Okay," Alec said. "How is that going to help me with the investigation?"

"Because he killed Penny." Her hands were gripped into fists at her side, and her cheeks turned red.

"What makes you think this?" he asked gently.

"Because he was seeing somebody else. I told Penny that she needed to leave him, but she wouldn't do it. They'd been married for a lot of years, and she felt like she would be abandoning him, but she should have done it. She'd still be alive now if she had."

"Who was he seeing?" Alec asked.

She glanced at me before continuing. "Dori Kellogg. The two of them have been having an affair for some time, from what I can tell. I don't know why Penny didn't open her eyes to this."

I had to hold my breath to keep from gasping. *Dori?* I couldn't believe it.

"How do you know they were seeing each other?" he asked.

She pursed her lips. "Because I saw them together at a restaurant in Milford a year ago. I told Penny about it, but she wouldn't believe me."

"Are they still seeing each other?" I asked.

She nodded. "Yes, they're still seeing each other. I've heard from other people in town that they've seen them out together. I'm just certain that he killed Penny to get rid of her so that he and Dori could be together. It wouldn't surprise me if he told Penny about the affair, and then she still refused to leave him. I don't know why she was such a sucker for him."

I wasn't sure what to make of all of this. I couldn't imagine Jonathan and Dori getting together, but Julia had seen them with her own eyes.

Alec nodded. "I'll look into this. Thank you for letting me know."

Julia sighed. "I hope you will. Something needs to be done about him if he's the killer. Now, if you'll excuse me, I've got to check on what's going on in the kitchen. Some people need constant supervision." She rolled her eyes. "It's good seeing the two of you. If you need to talk to me again about this, Alec, I'm here."

He nodded. "Thank you for the information, Julia. I'll call you if I need anything else."

When she was gone, I turned to Alec. "Well, it looks like it may be true, then. I'm stunned."

He nodded and picked his spoon up. "Sounds like it, doesn't it?"

And then I remembered something. "Dori made a comment at the party. She said there could be a new Mrs. Braxton next year."

He looked at me, spoon raised half-way to his mouth. "She said that?"

I nodded. "Right after Penny was taken away by ambulance."

"Really," he said. "That's interesting."

I was shocked to hear that Jonathan and Dori were having an affair. And I felt sorry for Penny. She had to have known that people were talking.

CHAPTER 9

The following day, I packed up some chocolate cupcakes, and Lucy and I drove over to Jonathan's house. It had only been three days since his wife had died, so I wasn't sure if he would even answer the door, let alone allow us to come inside and talk to him. But Jonathan had always been someone who I considered to be very open and friendly. If he was home, chances were good he would talk to us.

I knocked on the door, and when no one answered, we waited a couple of minutes, and then I tried again. Jonathan answered the door after the second knock, looking haggard, with dark circles beneath his eyes.

"Jonathan, we're so sorry for your loss," I said

kindly. "We wanted to stop by and check on you. How are you doing?"

He shook his head, and tears welled up in his eyes. "Not good. I still can't get over the fact that Penny is gone."

"I'm so sorry," Lucy said. "I know this is so hard."

He nodded and swallowed. "Never in a million years did I ever imagine that something like this would happen to Penny. To both of us, because without her, I am nothing."

He seemed to be genuinely upset about Penny's death, in spite of the fact that two people had said he was cheating on her. Maybe these were tears of regret. "I'm so sorry. I know it's not much, but I made some cupcakes for you." I held up the box.

He smiled sadly. "Penny was so excited when she asked you to make the desserts for the garden party. She told me that night she couldn't believe you said yes on such short notice."

I was surprised to hear this. Penny was the kind of woman that you didn't say no to. "I'm so glad I could make her happy then."

His eyes widened. "Oh, where are my manners? Would you ladies like to come inside?"

I nodded. "Yes, if it won't be a bother for you."

"It's no bother. Come on in."

We followed him inside the house. It looked the

same as I remembered. Nothing had changed since the morning of the garden party. He showed us to the living room, and we sat down on the couch across from him. I set the box of cupcakes on the coffee table. "Jonathan, you're not trying to get through this alone, are you?" The house was quiet, and I wondered about it.

He slumped back on the loveseat and shook his head. "No, my sons will be here this afternoon. One lives in Buffalo and the other in San Diego. We're going to plan the funeral when they get here and try to give their mother a proper send-off. I laughed to myself as I thought about the funeral. If Penny had planned it, she would have done it up big. Loads and loads of flowers and plants, and she would be dressed in a leopard print velvet dress. She loved her leopard prints. There's a dress in her closet we bought while in Paris twenty years ago that she rarely got the chance to wear because we didn't have the right events to attend where she could wear something like that. Well, she's going to wear it for her funeral, along with some amber stone jewelry that she bought to go with the dress."

I smiled. "That sounds wonderful. I'm sure that if she knew how much thought and care you were putting into her funeral, it would make her happy."

Lucy nodded. "I bet she's looking down on you

now, just so excited that you know exactly what she would like."

He smiled. "I think you're right. I think she knows exactly what's going on, and she will be thrilled about the funeral." He turned to me. "I haven't talked to Alec for a couple of days. Does he have any idea who killed my wife yet?"

"I don't know that he's ready to arrest anybody just yet, but you can be assured that he's working very hard on this case. Jonathan, do you have any idea who might have killed your wife?" I hoped that he had suddenly thought of somebody that he hadn't thought of at the very beginning when Alec first interviewed him.

He gazed at me and sighed. "It had to be Dori Kellogg. There's nobody else who would kill her."

I hesitated and tried not to show my surprise. Both Dori and Penny competed with their gardens, hoping for more attention than the other. The garden society didn't have much of an award, just a classic trophy dipped in gold, and I suppose there were bragging rights. Those bragging rights must've meant the world to both Dori and Penny. But Julia Desmond had said he was having an affair with Dori.

"Why do you think Dori would kill her?" I asked when I regained my composure.

"You know how the two of them were together.

They were at one another all the time. I told Penny to ignore her, but she refused. Sometimes Dori would call her up late at night in the early spring and taunt her, telling her that her flowers were so much better than Penny's." He chuckled. "It made Penny so angry. I told her I didn't understand why she was putting up with this. Why didn't she just ignore her? But she let it get to her."

"Then why did Penny invite Dori to her garden party?" Lucy asked.

"She wanted her to see how much nicer her garden was than Dori's. You know what they say, 'Keep your friends close, and your enemies closer.' She wanted to brag and show off that garden, and she wanted to keep an eye on Dori and see what her reaction would be. She hoped to gauge the success of her garden by Dori's reaction."

"She wanted to put fear in her, didn't she?" I asked. It seemed like a silly game to play, but if Dori really was that competitive, then I wondered if Dori could have killed Penny. But what about the relationship he had with Dori?

He nodded. "She certainly did. And to be honest, I think Penny's garden was much better than Dori's."

I studied his face as he spoke. He had to be lying, didn't he? "Jonathan, why did Penny have Wolfsbane growing right there on her patio?"

He shook his head. "I don't know how it got there."

"What?" I asked. "It was right there. It was one of the first plants that we noticed because it was so beautiful."

"Yeah, I was thinking I wanted some to plant in my yard until I heard what it was," Lucy said.

He nodded. "It's in a pot, and it's usually out in the garden. But somebody moved it up to the patio. Penny thought it was a beautiful plant and insisted on growing some. I told her it was dangerous, but she insisted she would be careful with it."

Lucy and I turned to look at each other, then I turned back to him. "Did you tell Alec this?"

He shook his head. "No, because I didn't even realize it was there until this morning. I thought maybe one of the officers who were here looking for evidence had moved it during the investigation. But you saw it there on the day of the party?"

We both nodded. "Yes, it was right there. We talked to your mother about it," Lucy said. "The flowers on that plant are absolutely gorgeous in color. It's a striking flower."

He looked at Lucy. "My mother was talking about it?"

Lucy nodded. "She explained to us what it was, and what it did. We thought it was a little odd that there was a poisonous plant right there on the patio, where the party was going to be held."

I leaned forward slightly. It was odd that he didn't notice it on the patio. Who moved it there? "Yes, your mother told us what the plant was. We wouldn't have known unless she told us. We've got to talk to Alec and let him know the pot was moved on the morning of the party."

"I bet the killer's fingerprints are on the pot," Lucy said.

Jonathan shook his head slowly. "I can hardly believe it. The killer moved the pot."

I nodded and got my phone from my purse. This was exciting information. If Alec could get fingerprints from the pot, then we would know who the killer was.

CHAPTER 10

"What do you think of that?"

I turned to look at Lucy as I started my car. "I don't know what to think about that. Julia Desmond said that Jonathan was having an affair with Dori. But clearly, he's grieving for his wife. Would a man who is cheating on his wife really and truly grieve for her that way?"

She was quiet for a few moments as I pulled away from the curb, then she turned to look at me. "Would a man who is having an affair kill his wife?"

"It's happened before. I mean, they have to be some kind of psycho or something."

"If he's a psycho of some sort, and we don't know for sure whether or not he is, then certainly he could fake grieving for his wife, couldn't he?"

I nodded without looking at her. "Yes, of course. He could very well be faking the whole thing. It's not like we haven't run into people who have lied and faked whatever they needed to get us to believe their story." Lucy and I had dealt with a lot of liars and fakes in the past handful of years, so if Jonathan was faking his tears, it wouldn't be a surprise. Except that I felt like I knew Jonathan well enough to know that he was being genuine. I hoped I wouldn't be disappointed in that belief.

"You know what I just thought of?"

I shook my head. "No, what?"

"When we were there at the party, Elise Donovan and Penny were having a discussion. It seemed like Elise was very unhappy with Penny."

I nodded, thinking back. "Yes, Elise seemed upset about something, didn't she? She said 'it wasn't right', and whatever it was, it had something to do with something Penny had done."

"Maybe we should drop in on Elise and see if she'll tell us what that conversation was about."

I smiled. "I like the way you think, Lucy."

I made a left on Grant Avenue and headed to the pet store Elise owned.

* * *

WE STEPPED inside the pet store and the smell of sawdust shavings hit me. Elise had a variety of animals for sale, along with puppies and kittens that were being adopted out by the county shelter. I glanced at them and saw a handful of kittens playing together in a large enclosure, and puppies scampered around in a playpen.

"Oh, aren't they adorable," Lucy said. "I wish we had room for a puppy."

I glanced at the adjacent playpen that had six puppies of varying sizes and breeds yipping and yapping and playing happily.

I smile. "I've never been a dog person, but those puppies sure are cute."

We hurried over to look.

"Look at that little white one," she said, pointing through the glass. "She sure is cute. And I bet she won't get very big."

"She's adorable. I think you need a puppy, Lucy." The little dog had curly hair and a tan spot on her back, and one just above her right eye. She was having a ball with the other dogs.

She sighed. "I wonder what Ed would do if I just brought her home?"

"The only way to find out is to do it." I may have been encouraging my friend to do something that might have caused a little marital strife, but Lucy deserved a dog if she really wanted it, and that puppy was beyond adorable.

She chuckled. "I better think about it before I act hastily."

"Okay, suit yourself. But somebody might come in here and scoop her up."

"Oh, now you're not playing fair," she said, frowning. "She really is adorable."

"Can I help you ladies with something?"

We both turned around to see Elise wearing a blue smock with her name stitched on the right side above the pocket.

She grinned. "Oh, I didn't realize it was you two. How are you both doing?"

I nodded. "We're admiring your puppies and kittens, Elise. They're absolutely adorable."

She nodded. "Aren't they? The county brings the puppies and kittens to be adopted out. We go through them pretty quickly. I think people would rather see them playing here in the shop than go to the shelter to adopt them."

"I think it's a great thing that you're doing," Lucy said. "That way, these little cuties get out of the shelter and can find a loving home."

"I could never sell purebred puppies from puppy mills," she said. "I wouldn't feel right about it. But I do sell some hamsters, mice, and gerbils. They're all from a reputable breeder."

I nodded. "Elise, how have you been since Penny died? I know it was a shock for everybody at the garden party."

She sobered. "I tell you, that was the last thing I would have expected to happen. I still can't get over the fact that Penny is dead."

"We feel the same way," I said. "Elise, we happened to overhear part of a conversation between you and Penny at the party. It sounded like you were angry about something she had done."

She looked at me. "Are you asking me this because you think I killed her?"

I chuckled and shook my head. "No, Elise, we don't think you killed her. We just wondered if something was going on in Penny's life that you were aware of that might lead us to the killer."

She nodded, crossing her arms in front of herself. "Well, I felt like Penny was taking advantage of the gardening society judges. She had invited them to the party, and it wasn't right. The judging was going to happen in two weeks, and they should have walked into her garden to do the judging without having prior knowledge of it."

"Wait a minute," Lucy said. "The judges were there at the party?"

She shook her head. "They hadn't arrived by the

time Penny fell ill, but they were invited. It's unethical, if you ask me. If they had shown up, they would have had all that time to wander around the garden and admire it. Maybe they would have noticed things they might not have noticed when they had a limited time, and that gave Penny an unfair advantage."

"I agree. That isn't right. I wonder if the judges would have shown up?" I mused.

She shrugged. "I don't know, but I wouldn't have been surprised. One judge is a real flake, and if you ask me, he enjoys the contestants giving him extra attention. Rumor has it that Penny sent him a flower arrangement from her garden." She rolled her eyes.

"What?" I asked incredulously. "Why on earth would she do that?"

"And why would he accept it?" Lucy asked. "It sounds as if she was trying to buy her way into that prize."

Elise nodded. "That's what I said. Nobody has as large a garden as Penny did. Frankly, I don't know of anybody who puts the kind of money into their garden that she did, either. She was pretty much a shoo-in to win the award, but it wasn't right. There was a time when the garden judging was a lot of fun. Almost anybody could enter their garden and hope to at least have a chance at winning, but not anymore. Not once Penny got involved."

"That was the largest garden I have ever seen," Lucy said. "It was beautiful. Absolutely breathtaking. I can't imagine even attempting to compete against it."

She nodded. "Exactly. Most people wouldn't even attempt it."

"But some people still do," I pointed out.

"That's right, some people still do. Dori Kellogg is probably the only person who really gives Penny a run for her money, but even so, Penny has won that award for the last six years in a row. The last person who took the prize away from her was Dori. Before that, Penny had won the award four years in a row, and I think it really stuck in her craw that there was an interruption there in the middle. She couldn't brag that she had won it ten years in a row, and someone like Penny liked to brag."

I nodded. "So, she and Dori had a real competition with one another?" I asked.

She nodded. "They sure did."

"Then why was Dori invited to the party?" Lucy asked.

She smiled. "Oh, Penny invited her every year. She wanted to rub her nose in what she had done with her garden."

"Do you have a garden, Elise?" I asked.

"Oh, yes, I have a lovely garden. And there was a time when I used to enter the competition. I won once, too. But there's no way I'd ever win it again. Not with Penny competing. Maybe now that she's gone..."

"Aren't there rules that both the judges, and the contestants have to follow?" I asked, thinking about the judges being invited to the party. I could see where it would upset the other contestants.

She nodded. "There certainly are. Or at least there were. You can ask to see the set of rules when you sign up, but I noticed a couple of years ago that the rules have changed, and nothing is being said about judges being invited to garden parties, where they might take a look at one of the gardens ahead of time. Or accepting flower arrangements from contestants. I tell you, it takes all the fun out of it."

"It sounds like it," I said. "So, I guess Penny didn't like you pointing out that it wasn't right for the judges to be invited to the party?"

She nodded. "She didn't like that one bit, but what do I care? I'm not a contestant anymore."

This was all very interesting. If Penny was bending the rules and getting away with it, I could see it ruffling some feathers.

We stayed and chatted with Elise for a bit longer and watched the puppies and kittens play. In the end, Lucy decided not to adopt the puppy in case it would upset Ed, but we had found out some interesting information about Penny and her garden party. If I had been a contestant and I had found out that she was sucking up to the judges by sending them flower arrangements and then inviting them to her party, it would make me angry. Very angry indeed.

CHAPTER 11

We couldn't keep what Jonathan had said about Dori to ourselves. It seemed unfathomable to me that he was seeing her on the sly, yet now he said that she might have killed his wife.

Lucy and I went through the drive-through at the Cup and Bean Coffee Shop and picked up iced coffees for ourselves and Alec, along with some chocolate chunk scones. Arriving empty-handed at the police station would be uncouth.

When we walked into the police station, we were greeted by Jim Taylor at the front desk. He grinned when he saw us. "Hey Allie! How are you doing today?"

I smiled and nodded. "I'm doing great, Jim. You?"

He smiled and then glanced at what was in my hands. It wasn't much because I had only brought enough for us and Alec. I frequently brought baked goods to the officers here at the station, and they knew when I showed up, chances were good they were going to get a treat. I was going to disappoint them today.

"I would've been doing better if I saw those pink bakery boxes you usually bring with you," he said sadly.

"Oh, I'm so sorry, Jim. I've got to get to baking and bring all of you wonderful police officers a treat, don't I?" I should have tucked the bags that held our scones into my purse. There was no use in torturing the man.

"I told her we needed to bring treats for you all," Lucy said, throwing me under the bus.

I shot her a look. She had said no such thing; she was just trying to look good to Jim.

Jim sighed dramatically. "That's okay, Allie. I guess I'll find a way to make it through my day, anyway."

"Aw, now I feel bad, Jim. I promise to bring you something in the next few days, okay? Does that make it up to you?" I shot Lucy another look.

He grinned. "Sure, that definitely makes up for it. Double points if you make something chocolate."

"I will absolutely make you something chocolate then," I said, grinning back. "Can we go on through?"

He nodded and pressed the buzzer. "Sure, go ahead."

"Thanks, Jim," I called over my shoulder as we headed through the door that led to the offices. When the door closed behind us, I glanced at Lucy. "You told me to bring something?"

She shrugged. "I want to make sure that my neighborhood is adequately patrolled, so I've got to put in a good word for myself, right?"

I snorted and knocked on Alec's door. When he hollered for us to come in, I pushed the door open. "Hey!"

He looked up from his laptop. "Hey!"

I chuckled and closed the short distance between us, leaned over, and kissed him. "We brought sustenance." I set the iced coffee down, and Lucy set down the small bag with his chocolate chunk scone in it.

His eyes widened. "You two are lifesavers. I was just wondering what I could coax out of the vending machine that would be edible."

"We got here just in time then," I said as we sat in the chairs in front of his desk. "We had to stop by and tell you we talked with Jonathan Braxton this morning." I watched him when I brought this up.

He took a long drag on the straw of his iced coffee and then looked at me. "And?"

I glanced at Lucy and turned back to him. "Well, according to several people, he's seeing Dori on the sly, right? And when we went to talk to him, he pointed his finger at Dori and said that she was his wife's killer." I looked at him, waiting for his reaction.

His eyebrows shot up. "Wait, he's blaming his lover for killing his wife?"

I nodded. "He is blaming his lover for killing his wife."

"Did he tell you he thought Dori was his wife's killer previously?" Lucy asked him.

He shook his head. "No, he told me he didn't know who might have killed his wife. I'm surprised to hear him say that his mistress is her killer. It's even more surprising that he didn't call me to tell me that if that's what he truly believes."

I nodded. "I think you'd better have another talk with him. I will say that he seems very sincere about his grief over his wife's passing, but if he's having an affair with Dori, as we believe, then he has to be faking his sincerity."

"He was very convincing," Lucy said, taking a sip of her iced coffee and nodding. "This is very good iced coffee. But I never would have thought that

Jonathan was faking his grief. He was crying and everything."

Alec was quiet as he opened the little paper bag to look at what we had brought him. He smiled when he saw the scone. "Now this looks tasty. Thanks for bringing the coffee and the scone." He looked up at us again. "It's odd that he's blaming Dori for his wife's murder. Maybe the two have had a falling out?"

"Maybe Dori tired of waiting for him to leave his wife, and she killed Penny," I said. "And now he's angry that she killed her."

Lucy nodded. "I bet that's it. Penny and Jonathan have two sons together, after all, and what decent human being would want to see their children's parent killed? Even if they don't want to be married to them anymore, they don't want their children's mother to be murdered, either."

Alec was quiet again for a moment and then took another sip of his iced coffee. "I was talking to a couple of other officers here, and it seems that a few months ago there was a call that came in about a disturbance at the Braxtons' house. It was between Penny and Arlene Braxton."

I gasped. "Seriously? Who made the call?"

"A neighbor. A couple of officers came out and talked with them. It appeared that the two women were arguing rather loudly out on the front doorstep.

Penny didn't want Arlene to come into the house, and Arlene wasn't about to leave simply because Penny demanded that she do so."

"That Arlene is spunky, isn't she?" Lucy said. "She reminds me of my grandmother."

I nodded. "And we still haven't sat down and talked with Arlene yet. We've got to do that. I can't believe that the police had to be called. Can you imagine the commotion that she must have been causing? In that neighborhood?"

Alec nodded. "Exactly. According to the neighbors, they were screaming at one another. Arlene told Penny she was sorry her son ever met her and that someday she would pay for the misery she had brought to her family."

"Oh," Lucy said, drawing the word out. "That sounds like a threat."

"Did the police do anything about it?" I asked. "They didn't drag Arlene down to jail, did they?"

He chuckled. "No, the woman needs a cane to get around. They didn't really take it as much of a threat at the time, to be honest, and I wouldn't have either. They talked to the two ladies and got them to settle down, and Arlene reluctantly went home."

"Can you imagine what the holidays must be like for that family?" I took another sip of my coffee. I was glad that my family got along. Having to go through holidays with two women screaming at one another would have been tough.

"I think I would have taken my holidays in the Bahamas if I had to deal with that," Lucy said. "That would be a lot more fun."

"That would be fun," I agreed. "If my family ever decides they don't like one another anymore, we may have to have our holidays in the Bahamas." I turned back to Alec. "Was that the only time they ever went out there?"

He shook his head. "I went back a few years in the reports and found two other times in the last three years that the police were called for disturbing the peace, but by the time they got there, no one was around. They knocked on the front door, and Penny told them they might have just had their TV up too loud."

"Oh, the old 'my television was turned up too loud' gag," I said, shaking my head. "But even though Arlene gets around with a cane, it certainly wouldn't have stopped her from poisoning Penny's tea and making sure that she got the right cup. It's not a very physical murder."

He nodded. "Agreed. I'll be having another talk with Arlene in the next day or two, even though I don't feel she could be the murderer. Jonathan is more of an interest to me now that you've told me he's blaming the murder on Dori Kellogg. I need to find out what his motive for that is."

I agreed with Alec. I felt like Jonathan was a better suspect than his mother. And then I thought of something. "Maybe the two of them acted together? Maybe they were both tired of Penny's shenanigans and spending so much money on her garden, and they got together and murdered her."

Lucy turned to look at me. "I bet you're right. Somebody had to make sure that Penny got the right cup of tea after all. If that cup had gone to the wrong person, they would have murdered an innocent bystander. She wouldn't have thought twice about Jonathan handing her a cup of tea to drink."

I took a sip of my iced coffee, taking this in. That was true. They had to be careful about what they did with that poisoned cup of tea. It would have been an even bigger tragedy if it had gone to somebody they didn't intend to kill.

We needed to speak to Arlene.

CHAPTER 12

The following day, Lucy and I stopped by Arlene's house to see how she was doing. I made some chocolate cupcakes with raspberry cream filling to take to her. I still owed the police officers cupcakes, but that would have to wait until later.

I turned to look at my adorable granddaughter, Lilly. She had at first stubbornly resisted learning to walk, but once she mastered it, she was constantly on the move. Currently, she was attempting to silently sneak up on Dixie, who was peacefully enjoying a midmorning snack from his food bowl.

"Now, Lilly, Dixie doesn't like it when you sneak up behind him." Dixie had the patience of a saint when it came to Lilly, but I still kept an eye on her to make sure she didn't pull his tail or ears.

Lilly didn't turn to me or even acknowledge me, but she did grin as she reached out for his tail. But something must have warned Dixie because he quickly twitched it away from her, wrapping it around himself. Dixie wasn't quite sure what to make of this little human who had invaded his world in recent months, but he was always gentle with her, and that was my biggest concern.

I picked Lilly up, swinging her onto my hip like I used to do with my kids when they were small, and then slung my purse over my opposite shoulder. "We are going to visit Mrs. Arlene Braxton, Lilly. I think your cuteness will get her to open up about things."

Lilly said something indistinguishable, and I picked up the small box of cupcakes for Arlene.

Lilly's babysitter had come down with a cold, and out of an abundance of caution, my daughter-in-law Sarah kept her home, which meant my home. That was fine. I didn't get enough time with Lilly, even though we kept her frequently. She was growing so fast, I knew it wouldn't be long before she would be in school, and I would see her less often.

I hurried out to my car, glancing up at the clouds forming above. The weatherman said we would get a late spring rain today, and I think he might have been correct about it.

After buckling Lilly into her car seat, I got behind

the wheel and started my car. We were going to pick up Lucy on the way over.

* * *

We pulled up to Arlene Braxton's house just as it started to sprinkle lightly. "Well, she had better let us in, or we're going to get wet," Lucy said as we got out of the car. She was holding the cupcakes, and I got Lilly out of her car seat, and we hurried up and onto the porch.

I knocked on the front door, and we waited. Arlene lived in an older neighborhood in Sandy Harbor. The homes were large and neatly kept here. I could just imagine what life must have been like in these homes in the 1920s when most of them were built.

Arlene opened the door and looked surprised to see us. "Oh, it's you, Allie? Lucy?"

I nodded. "Yes, good morning, Arlene. How are you doing? Lucy and I have been talking about dropping in to see you to see how you have been doing since that horrible tragedy happened with Penny."

She made a face. "I'd better put my glasses on; I can barely tell who you ladies are," she chuckled. "And who is that little lass you've got on your hip?"

I turned Lilly so she could get a better look at her.

"This is my granddaughter, Lilly. She is fifteen months old, full of sass, and always on the move, if you know what I mean."

She chuckled and nodded. "I sure do. Why don't you ladies come in?"

We followed her into the house, and she picked up her glasses from an end table and put them on. "There now, I can see all of you just fine. My goodness, but Miss Lilly sure is a beautiful little girl. Look at all that strawberry blond hair. Just lovely."

I smiled. "Thank you. I happen to think she is as well, and I know it's not just because I'm biased."

"Lilly is the sweetest little thing," Lucy agreed. "Allie made you some cupcakes, Arlene." She held out the small box.

"Well, will you look at that," Arlene said, smiling. "That is so sweet of you, Allie. You know I will enjoy every single one of them." She took the box from Lucy, and we all sat down. Lilly immediately spotted a long-haired gray cat on an end chair and wiggled to get down.

"Now, Lilly, that isn't our cat, and we don't know if he likes little girls," I said.

Arlene waved a dismissive hand. "That's Oscar. Oscar loves everyone. She can pet him if she wants to."

I released Lilly to hopefully not wreak havoc on the poor sleeping Oscar.

"How have you been, Arlene?" I asked gently. "We've been thinking about you."

She sat back in her seat. "Oh, I'm doing fine. It sure was a shock what happened to Penny, wasn't it? Not that I would blame anybody for wanting to poison her, of course, but it was still shocking, nonetheless." She chuckled lightly.

I shook my head. "What do you mean, not that you would blame anyone for poisoning her?"

She sighed, putting her slipper-clad feet on the coffee table. "Penny was just an awful person. I know it's not polite to speak ill of the dead, but I've got to tell the truth, right? She was self-centered and caused so much trouble for my family. She was always so critical of everybody and lied to them about one another, trying to stir up trouble." She made a clucking sound with her tongue and shook her head. "I don't know what gets into some people. Why do they have to be so awful?"

Lucy shook her head. "I don't know, but it seems like some people just like to cause trouble, doesn't it?"

She nodded. "They sure do. Allie, I know your husband is investigating the murder. I talked to him a few days ago, too. Has he found her killer?"

I shook my head. "No, not yet. But he will find

them soon. Do you have any thoughts about who might have wanted to kill her?"

She shook her head as she looked at Lilly, who was gently petting Oscar. The cat had woken up and stretched his back out for her, purring loudly. "Well, like I told your husband, the only person who really would have had anything against her, at least bad enough to kill her, would be her so-called best friend, Rebecca Adams. I know what you're thinking: they were friends, right? Why would she want to kill her? But sometimes people just pretend to be friends, if you know what I mean."

I nodded. "Yes, I know that does sometimes happen. But did you see anything specific that made you think they weren't really friends? Or something that made you think Rebecca might have wanted to kill her?"

She shrugged. "All I know is that Rebecca was constantly making faces at Penny behind her back. It's like she was too scared to confront her when she said something hateful to her, so she would make a face at her when she wasn't looking. And I happen to know that when they were young, there was a boy they were both interested in. Penny lied to him about Rebecca, saying that she was fooling around with other boys. This was back when they were in high school, and that kind of thing was frowned upon back then, or at least more so than it is now. I don't know what all Penny told him, but she ended up with that boy, and I have a hunch that Rebecca never forgave her. I know about this because that boy was my brother's stepson. If I had known back then that she would set her cap for my son later, I would have said more to Jonathan about her, and he'd have been warned off."

"So, you've known Penny a long time, then?" I asked.

She nodded. "I certainly have. That woman was no good right from the beginning." She chuckled. "I guess I sound terrible, but the truth is the truth."

This was interesting, but not grounds for murder, in my opinion. "It's strange that she was poisoned with Wolfsbane," I said, wanting to approach this delicately. "That was the same plant that was on her patio. Why would she keep a poisonous plant on her patio?"

She shrugged. "I do not know. Honestly, I was a little surprised to see it sitting there, but then I thought, Penny's an idiot, so why should I be surprised?"

"So, it wasn't usually there?" Lucy asked.

She shook her head. "I really don't remember seeing it there before, but it could have been there. It's not like I hung around her house often, if you know what I mean."

"You told us about Wolfsbane right before the party started," I said. "Don't you find it odd that somebody made it into a tea and killed her that morning?"

"Odd?" She narrowed her eyes at me. "What are you trying to say, Allie?"

I shrugged. "I'd never really thought about Wolfsbane before that morning."

She shook her head. "I did not make Wolfsbane into a tea and kill my daughter-in-law if that's what you're asking. I kind of wish I had thought of such a thing, but I didn't."

Lucy snorted. "You don't mean that."

She nodded. "I do."

I gazed at her. It was clear she wasn't going to hide the fact that she couldn't stand Penny, but did she have it in her to kill her? It didn't appear so, but I had been wrong before.

"Do you think that Rebecca really had it in her to kill Penny after all these years? I mean, girls fight over boys. It's just one of those things. Why would she kill her now? After all these years?" I asked.

Arlene hesitated and then shook her head. "I have no idea. Honestly, if it wasn't her, then I don't know who it could be."

"Sometimes you just get a feeling about something," Lucy said.

"That's exactly right. I might not know what the reason is, but I have a hunch. A very strong hunch." Arlene smiled.

I nodded, not quite knowing what to make of Arlene. Had she killed her daughter-in-law and was just trying to blame Rebecca? Her reasons for accusing her were flimsy at best. We stayed and visited a while longer, and then I gathered up Lilly before she could drive Oscar to distraction.

CHAPTER 13

After talking to Arlene for a bit, I took Lucy back home. We both still wondered about Arlene, and whether she could be Penny's killer, but in my heart, I had to think that it wasn't her. She seemed honest. It would have been easy for her to pretend that she and Penny were close after she died to keep anyone from thinking she might have killed her, but she hadn't even bothered. It seemed that there was an awful lot of drama between the two women over the years, but did it mean she wanted to get rid of her daughter-in-law by any means necessary? I didn't think so.

After dropping Lucy off, I stopped by the grocery store and picked up a few things. I still needed to make some cupcakes for the officers at the station, and I was low on sugar, so I picked up ten pounds of that, along with a handful of other items that we needed. Lilly enjoyed the trip, sitting in the front of the cart and soaking up the attention of other shoppers, as well as the checker who rang us up.

"You are becoming quite the little ham, aren't you?" I said to her as I pushed my shopping buggy to the car. Lilly squealed. It was nearing lunchtime, and even though her mood was great now, I knew if we didn't get home soon and get her something to eat, there was going to be a tantrum. And the last thing I wanted was a toddler on a tear.

I parked the shopping cart, hit the button to release the trunk, and pushed it open. I only had three bags of groceries, which I quickly set into the trunk, and just as I was getting ready to close it, I realized somebody was behind me. Having heard so many horror stories of cute babies being stolen, I reached out and put my hand on Lilly's back before turning around. To my relief, I saw Gemma Anderson standing there.

She smiled at me. "Oh, I didn't mean to startle you, Allie. Is that your grandbaby? She sure is pretty."

I smiled back. Gemma went to school with my daughter, and although they weren't particularly close, I knew who she was, and we frequently said hello when we saw each other out and about.

"Good morning, Gemma. Yes, this is Thad's daughter, Lilly. She's fifteen months old, and she is full of spunk this morning," I responded.

Lilly giggled as if understanding we were talking about her.

Gemma smiled at her. "Well, aren't you the cutest little thing? You look just like your daddy."

"Doesn't she though?" I agreed.

She nodded. "She does." She looked at me. "Allie, is your husband working on Penny Braxton's murder case?"

I nodded, my hand reflexively grabbing for my sunglasses as Lilly reached for them as they hung from my purse. "Yes, he's working on that case. Why do you ask?"

She hesitated, crossing her arms in front of herself. "Well, I work for the Braxtons, you know."

I shook my head. "No, I didn't know. What kind of work do you do for them?"

She sighed, looking embarrassed now. "I'm their housekeeper. Or, I mean, I'm one of their housekeepers. Their house is so huge it takes more than one of us. But I'm working my way through college, and I needed a job. It's only part-time, just about twenty-five hours a week, but it's the perfect job for me. I go to school at night."

"I'm sure cleaning a house is hard work, but since

you're going to college, it will be temporary work, right?" I could tell she didn't particularly enjoy being called a housekeeper, but there was no need for her to be embarrassed. It was honest work, and I was sure the Braxtons treated her well.

She nodded. "Yes, I'm studying to be a nurse. That's all I've ever wanted to do with my life, and I'm happy to do this kind of work until I can graduate and hopefully get hired at one of the hospitals in the area."

I nodded. "Being a nurse is a fantastic career choice. It takes a special person to do that kind of work, and I know it will be a great fit for you." I wondered why she brought up the investigation but didn't want to ask just yet. Allowing a person to talk often yielded fruit. Ripe, juicy fruit.

She grinned. "My mother said that I was always so good at helping people when I was little. She said I was always concerned with my little friends if they scraped their knees or something. I felt like I was born to be a nurse."

I smiled, glancing at Lilly as she became restless. If I didn't get her home and get something for her to eat, she was going to have a full-blown tantrum soon. "I bet you'll be the perfect nurse."

She nodded. "Allie, there's something that I wanted to say to you, but I'm not sure how to go about it. Actually, I really wanted to say it to your husband, but, well," she said, glancing behind her.

My Spidey senses were tingling now. "Oh? What is it? You can talk to me."

She turned back to me and smiled uncomfortably. "Well, I hate to stick my nose where it doesn't belong. My mother was always a stickler for not tattling. She said it would get me into trouble." She tucked a strand of brown hair behind her ear and chuckled, but it sounded forced. "Gosh, what difference does it make what my mother told me?" She laughed.

I shook my head. "What's going on, Gemma? What did you need to tell me?"

She took a deep breath and breathed out slowly. "Well, like I said, I don't want to stick my nose into anybody else's business, but when I was cleaning up after the garden party, I came across a broken teacup." She looked at me meaningfully, and my heart started pounding in my chest.

"A broken teacup? Like the one that Penny may have been holding when she collapsed?"

She hesitated. "Well, that's the thing. I don't know if it's the one she was holding when she collapsed. I was inside the house when all the excitement began. I didn't even realize anything was going on until I heard the sirens coming to the house. I was inside, working on the finger sandwiches and other foods that Penny wanted to serve to her guests. You can imagine how surprised I was when the ambulance showed up."

I nodded. "Yes, it was a surprise to everyone that she had collapsed. And it's just terrible that she died the way she did. But this teacup? Where did you find it?"

"Out on the patio."

The patio? I had to keep my composure. "Where is it now? What happened to the teacup?"

She hesitated, glancing over her shoulder again, but nobody was standing near us to overhear our conversation. She turned back to me. "Mr. Braxton told me to throw it away. I told him it might be important. See, we didn't do any cleaning until after Penny had died. Everyone was in shock, and Mr. Braxton insisted we serve the guests, thinking she was going to feel better right away and return to the party. But most people left right after she was taken to the hospital, and Mr. Braxton called from the hospital and told us to take a break and come back at two o'clock to clean up."

I smiled sadly. "I'm sure her death was unexpected."

She nodded. "We all thought she would be fine. But when we returned to the house to clean up, Mr. Braxton was already there, and he said she had passed. We felt terrible. I went out to clean the patio, and that was when I pointed the cup out to Mr. Braxton and told him that maybe the police needed that cup since at that time, we were told there was a possibility she had been murdered, and one of the girls had told me Penny was drinking from that cup when she collapsed. He told me I was being silly and to just clean it up and throw it away. But I overheard your husband talking to Mr. Braxton the following day, and he said that it could have been poisoning."

My heart dropped. "And did you clean it up and throw it away?"

She shook her head. "I swept it up and put it into a bag. I heard later that the police came to search the house and the patio. But by that time, everything had been cleaned up and put away. I wanted to tell your husband about the cup, but Mr. Braxton told me not to. And if he finds out I gave the teacup to the police, I might lose my job."

I stared at her, wanting to scream at her. "Where is the teacup?" I asked calmly.

"It's in the trunk of my car," she said. "I put it into a bag and saved it, but if Mr. Braxton finds out I gave this to the police, I might lose my job. I need that money to pay for college."

I nodded. "Will you give me the teacup? I'll tell

Alec not to let on to Mr. Braxton that you gave it to us. This cup may be very important to the case."

She tilted her head. "My car's over here."

I nodded and picked Lilly up out of the shopping cart, closed my trunk, and followed her two aisles over to her car. Gemma unlocked her trunk, picked up a small paper bag with the top folded over, and handed it to me. "It's in here. Like I said, I really don't know if it was the cup that Penny was drinking out of or not. The poison might not have even been put in her tea, right?"

I nodded. "Yes, we don't know how she got a hold of the poison. It may have been earlier in the morning, and probably was," I said, remembering that she had been sneezing and seemed to be unsteady on her feet when Lucy and I first arrived at her house. "But this could be a very important piece of evidence. Thank you so much for bringing it to my attention and giving it to me. I promise Alec will not tell Mr. Braxton that you gave it to us."

She nodded. "Thank you. I don't enjoy working for the Braxtons, if you want to know the truth. But I also don't like that somebody murdered Penny, and I couldn't just stand by and do nothing if this is the teacup the poison was given to her in."

"Why didn't you bring it to my attention earlier?" I asked before turning away.

She hesitated and shrugged. "I was scared. I'm sorry. I should have given it to you earlier."

I nodded. "Gemma, when Mr. Braxton told you his wife might have been murdered, did he give any indication that he thought it was true?"

"Yes, he said it was a ridiculous thought and he was sure it would turn out that she had some sort of medical issue."

I smiled. "Thank you for giving the cup to me." I headed back to my car, and after putting Lilly in her car seat, I set the bag on the floorboard of the passenger side and headed back to the police station. I hoped this teacup would give us the last piece of evidence that we needed to figure out who killed Penny.

CHAPTER 14

Alec was delighted that we now had the teacup that Penny Braxton was drinking from when she collapsed. Or at least, we hoped that this was the same teacup, and we hoped that the poison was put into this cup. If it was, there might be fingerprints on the cup, and if the poison was indeed served in the tea, we might be able to follow the trail back to whoever had their hands on that teacup first.

Lucy and I sat across from Mr. Winters at the Cup and Bean. "So, Mr. Winters, have you found out anything about the case?" Sometimes Mr. Winters came up with some significant leads in a case, and I hoped that was the case today, no pun intended.

He folded over his newspaper. "Well, lots of

people didn't like Penny Braxton, but I suppose that doesn't come as any surprise, does it?"

I shook my head. "No, I guess it isn't a surprise. Did you learn anything in particular about her?"

He shrugged. "She didn't treat people nicely. Or at least she didn't treat some people nicely. I guess when you make a lot of money, you can choose who to be kind to." He looked at me, one eyebrow raised.

"Well, it shouldn't be that way, but I suppose it is sometimes," Lucy conceded. She picked up her blueberry crumble latte and took a sip.

He nodded. "Exactly. I would hope that I would not become a mean person if I were suddenly handed a few million dollars. But nobody has ever seen fit to hand me a few million dollars, so I suppose we will never know for sure." He chuckled.

I shook my head. "Mr. Winters, I could never see you becoming a mean person."

"Well, thank you, Allie. I appreciate the vote of confidence. But I heard something." He leaned in. "Priscilla Cortland used to be one of the judges for the garden society until a few years ago. They were going to award first place to Dori Kellogg, but then suddenly, the other three judges changed their minds and wanted to give it to Penny. They wouldn't tell her why they had changed their minds, only saying that Penny had the nicer garden and deserved to win. This made her angry because she felt it wasn't true. At that time, Penny's garden wasn't as large and didn't have the variety of plants that it has now. She realized Penny had to have bribed them, and when she accused the other judges of this, they denied it and said she was crazy. She quit the society after that."

"Wow," I said and glanced at Lucy.

She shook her head. "Wow, is right."

My head was spinning. "Think about what that would have done to Dori if she was aware she was supposed to win."

"She knew," Mr. Winters said. "Priscilla told her a year later. She said she was so angry about it, she couldn't keep it to herself."

I sat back in my seat, taking this in. Was Dori our killer? I looked at the two of them. "I have something to say, but I can't give you details, because I was sworn to secrecy." They both turned to me. "We may have the teacup the poison was served in. I say 'may' because we don't know for sure."

Lucy gasped. "Really? How did you come by it?"

I shook my head. "That's part of what I've been sworn to secrecy about, and I can't explain now. You'll just have to take my word for it. I have to keep the details to myself for now."

She nodded. "All right. I won't pry for details. At least not yet."

"We don't know if it's the cup or if the poison was even in it for sure yet. Alec has sent it off to the lab and put a rush on it." I took a sip of my coffee.

I glanced up as I caught someone headed in our direction out of the corner of my eye. I smiled, my heart speeding up. "Good morning, Dori."

She nodded. "Good morning to all of you. I just happened to notice you all sitting over here and thought I would say hello. Allie, what's going on with the murder case? Has Alec made an arrest yet?" She took a sip from her cup.

I shook my head. "No, he hasn't yet. But I'm sure it's coming soon." I watched her face for her reaction, but it was blank.

She nodded and sat down in the chair next to Mr. Winters without asking, setting her cup of coffee on the table. "I've been thinking this over. I can't say that Penny and I were close because we weren't. She bragged about that garden of hers," she said, rolling her eyes. "Believe me, every time I ran into her around town, that's all I heard about. That woman was so full of herself and that garden, but everybody knows she didn't do any actual work out there. She just told the gardeners what to do, and they did it. Now I, on the other hand, actually work in my garden, and I'm quite proud of it. Yes, I get some help, but I do as much work as I am capable of since I am retired. I retired very early, so I spend a good portion of each day out there."

Dori seemed to have something important to say, but she was beating around the bush. "I didn't realize you had retired. I guess it gives you a lot of time to work in your garden, doesn't it?" I said.

She nodded. "My husband says I'm obsessed, but one man's obsession is another woman's passion." She laughed, even though I wasn't quite sure what that meant.

"You must have a beautiful garden," Lucy said. "Would you mind if we came and looked at it sometime? I sure admire people who have the time and inclination to make their garden beautiful."

She nodded. "Of course. You all come by anytime you want, and I'll give you a tour. Mr. Winters, would you like to come too?"

He nodded. "I'd be delighted, of course. I have a few rosebushes at my house, but not much else. As Lucy said, it's nice to see when somebody puts a lot of effort into their garden. And since you compete in that garden society contest, I'm sure that your garden is beautiful. I bet it's award-winning."

She glanced at him, then nodded again. "You better believe it. I worked hard on it, and I should have won the last several years, just for the fact that I'm the one who does most of my own work. I mean, how can you enter a gardening competition when you don't do any gardening?" She rolled her eyes.

I nodded. "You've got a point there, Dori. You said you were thinking about things. Did you mean you were thinking about who killed Penny? Who do you think did it? Everybody has an opinion on it, and I'd love to hear yours."

She sighed. "Well, if I had to take a wild guess who would have killed her, I would have to say that it was her mother-in-law, Arlene Braxton. Those two were like oil and water. They couldn't get along for anything."

"But Arlene is quite elderly," I pointed out. "Do you really think she would have killed her daughter-in-law? I mean, what was the point? She's suffered with her all these years, so why kill her now?"

She nodded. "That's true. She has put up with her all these years, but from what I could see, their disgust with one another only worsened over the years. It seems like Jonathan did little to mend the rift between them."

"Oh?" I asked. "I would have thought that he would have wanted to see his wife and his mother get along. If only for the sake of their children, even though they're adults now. They've all got to spend time together during the holidays."

She nodded, leaning in. "Right? I mean, why not

do everything you could to make them happy? I'll never understand it. But then, I'm not one of those people who tries to step in and cause trouble for others. That's something I don't understand either. Why can't people just get along?"

"That's a question for the ages," Lucy added. "Some people just can't seem to get along with anyone."

She took a sip of her coffee. "And that's exactly the thing. I think that both Arlene and Penny were troublesome people to get along with. It seems like they were never happy, especially with one another."

"You said you didn't think Jonathan helped the situation between his mother and wife," I said. "How do you know that? And what about his and Penny's marriage? Do you know how that was? Were they happy?" I watched her face carefully, and she looked up, our eyes meeting. She frowned almost imperceptibly before answering.

"Well, I'm afraid I wouldn't know about that. It is their business, right? The two of them are probably the only ones who could answer that question." She looked away and took another sip of her coffee, then looked at me again. "But if I were your husband, I would definitely talk with Arlene. It's not like Penny was beaten to death or shot or anything like that.

How hard is it to mix a little poison into her tea or her food? Anybody could do that."

I gazed at her. "Why do you think the poison was mixed into her tea?" As far as I knew, that wasn't something that had gotten around, although everybody at the garden party saw her drinking a cup of tea. Maybe she was making an assumption, or maybe she knew because she was the one who put it there. And she didn't answer my question about how she knew Jonathan hadn't helped smooth things over with Arlene and Penny's relationship.

She shrugged, looking surprised that I would even ask the question. "Well, it could have been put in anything. Like I said, it could have been mixed into her food. But you know, tea is rather bitter to begin with, and maybe it hid the taste of the poison. I really don't know. Didn't they test the tea served at the garden party?"

I shrugged. "I don't really know. Alec doesn't go into detail with me about investigations. He'll tell me some things, but there's an awful lot that he keeps to himself. You know how those detectives are."

I was looking at the killer. I was almost certain of it.

She nodded slowly and suddenly stood to her feet. "Well, it's been nice talking to you, ladies, and Mr.

Winters. I've got so much running around to do today. Stop by whenever you want to look at my garden. Or better yet, call me first to make sure I'm home. I feel like I spend almost as much time out running errands for my husband as I do at home in my garden. But I would be more than pleased to have you all look at it."

"We would love to," I said. "Have a good day, Dori."

We watched as she headed out the coffee shop door, and when it closed behind her, I turned to Lucy. "Well."

Lucy nodded. "Well, indeed."

"Well, what?" Mr. Winters asked.

"Well, it's rumored that she's having an affair with Jonathan Braxton." I gave him a look.

"Oh," he said, nodding in understanding. "I see. Well, indeed."

I wondered if her interest in the case was because she was the killer, and she wanted to know whether Alec was getting ready to make an arrest. In fact, I was almost certain of it.

CHAPTER 15

The following morning, Lucy and I went for a run in one of Sandy Harbor's most elite neighborhoods. The houses here were beautiful and large, most built within the last twenty years or so. But these weren't your average cookie-cutter homes, the style of which plagued many more modern neighborhoods. No, these were custom-built homes, and each had a different façade picked out by the homeowners. If you wanted to live in this neighborhood, you had better bring your checkbook.

"I wish I had the money to live in a neighborhood like this," Lucy huffed as we ran.

I nodded. "These are beautiful homes, aren't they? But you know me. I prefer older homes. They have more character."

"That's true. But I sure like modern amenities, and I bet every one of these homes is stuffed with modern amenities."

She had a point. If you had a home built in this neighborhood, then you had some money, and there was no way these homeowners were going to skimp on the fun and fancy things that made a house special. I had heard some of these homes were built with home theaters. Alec had suggested that we could turn our ballroom into a home theater, but I loved the ballroom, and on the rare occasion we entertained, I wanted it to be available. Our house had been a fixer-upper, and we had gotten it for a steal after Lucy and I found a dead body in it.

As we ran along the gently sloping streets, I took in the sights. Most of the homes had unbelievably green lawns that were neatly kept, with each blade of grass exactly the same height as the next. I didn't see many vehicles parked out front. I was quite certain those expensive vehicles were tucked away neatly in their four-car garages.

As we ran, I saw a familiar figure halfway down the block. I nudged Lucy, and she looked in the direction that I nodded, and she nodded back.

We hurried a little faster as Rebecca Adams got out of her expensive SUV idling in her driveway. She had just backed it out of her garage and must have forgotten something because she left the door open and was heading toward her house. She was dressed in a tennis outfit, her blond hair held out of her face with a wide hair band.

"Good morning, Rebecca!" I called.

She turned and looked in our direction, eyebrows raised, probably not expecting anybody out at this early hour.

Then she smiled when she recognized us. "Good morning, Allie, good morning, Lucy. Fancy meeting you two out here this early in the morning."

I nodded, and we came to a stop in front of her. "Right? Lucy and I decided we'd better get our run in early. It's supposed to get warm today, and I would rather run while it's still cool."

She nodded, smiling. "That's exactly what I'm going to do, only I am going to play tennis. Not that you couldn't tell." She laughed, looking down at her tennis dress.

"Where are you going to play tennis?" Lucy asked.

"The country club. Where else?" She chuckled. "My husband insists we remain active members of the country club, even though I really don't care for it much. But they have some excellent tennis courts there."

"I've never been to the country club. I used to play tennis in high school, but it's been eons since I even attempted it. It is a lot of fun though," I said, nodding and leaning back against her SUV. It was gold-colored, and if I wasn't mistaken, it must have cost close to a hundred thousand dollars.

She smiled sadly. "Penny and I loved to play tennis at the country club, and it breaks my heart a little that I'm not going to play with her today. I have another friend who agreed to meet me there. She thought it might pull me out of the doldrums that I've been in since Penny died."

"It's good for you to get out," Lucy agreed. "When you lose somebody who you're close to, you need to get out of the house now and then to feel a bit more human."

She nodded. "I feel the same way." She turned to me. "Any news on whether the killer is going to be arrested soon?"

I shook my head. "No, not yet. You know how it is. These things take time, as Alec says every time I bring it up."

She crossed her arms in front of herself. "I found out about Dori and Jonathan." She rolled her eyes. "I can't believe he would do that to Penny. In the weeks before her death, Penny told me she suspected he was up to no good. But I have to admit that I brushed off the idea. Penny could be so dramatic, and I thought the two of them had probably just had a spat, and she was angry at him."

"So, she suspected he was cheating on her?" Lucy asked.

She nodded, frowning. "Yes, and not only that, but she told me that if something should happen to her, it would be Jonathan who did it. I wish I had listened to her."

I was surprised to hear this. "Wait, she thought Jonathan might hurt her? Or kill her?"

She sighed. "She didn't come right out and say he might kill her, but she said she was worried he might do something to hurt her. But Penny, like I said, was so dramatic. It was hard to take her seriously. I've known Jonathan for years, and I would never suspect something like that from him. Even after she was murdered, I still didn't believe it could be Jonathan. He just isn't that sort of person. But now that I've found out about him and Dori, I've changed my mind. I think maybe the two of them got together and murdered Penny so they could be together."

I shook my head. How could she be so calm about this? "Did you tell this to Alec?"

She shook her head. "Not yet. Like I said, I really didn't believe that Jonathan could have done such a thing, so I didn't feel like it was worth bringing up. But I saw Dori and Jonathan out having lunch yesterday, and now I am convinced that one or both of them did it. I feel like such a fool. I should have listened to Penny."

I was alarmed to hear that Penny had told Rebecca that if something should happen to her, it would be Jonathan who had done it. If Lucy had told me the same thing about Ed, and then she turned up dead, the first thing I would have told the police was that she was worried he would do something. Lucy and I stared at her in shock.

She shook her head. "I know. I know exactly what you're thinking. I was so stupid. As soon as I'm done with my tennis game, I'm going by the police station to talk to your husband. I just can't believe I could be so foolish."

"I think it's incredibly important that you talk to him about this," I agreed. "Alec won't be in the office until 8:00, so you have time for your tennis game."

She nodded. "The worst thing about all of this is that Penny and I told one another everything. And when I say everything, I mean *everything*. We always talked things over, and here she told me who her killer was going to be, and I ignored it. I am just beside myself; I feel like I've betrayed my very best friend. I wish I had encouraged her to leave him so that she could have been safe." She shook her head, and tears sprang to her eyes.

"But you said that she was dramatic," Lucy pointed out. "I guess if a person is always crying wolf, it's hard to believe them when it's something important."

Rebecca nodded. "That's exactly right, but still. I should have taken this more seriously. But she did cry wolf quite a bit. And now I wonder what else she told me that I dismissed and should have paid attention to. Maybe I would have seen the signs of this years ago. I just feel terrible about it."

I sighed. "Rebecca, don't beat yourself up too much. We all make mistakes, and ultimately the decision as to whether she would leave her husband was up to her. She was a mature woman who should have left him if she truly felt that he would do her harm." I wasn't sure I believed my own words. If Penny had been afraid of Jonathan, she may have been too scared to leave him. Maybe she thought it was safer if she stayed there in the house until she could figure out what to do.

"I suppose," she said, sighing. "Well, thanks for listening to me drone on. I've been so preoccupied with this, that I completely forgot my tennis racket inside the house. I was just going to run in and get it, and then I've got to get to the country club. I don't want to have my friend worrying about me. Please let your husband know I will be dropping by the police station at around 8:30 a.m. to talk to him about this. And I really appreciate you both listening."

I smiled and nodded. "Anytime, Rebecca. Just give me a call if you ever need to talk."

Lucy and I continued our run while she went into her house to retrieve her tennis racket.

"I would feel terrible if my best friend had told me something, and I had dismissed it, and then she ended up dead," Lucy said.

I nodded. "Me too. That's just awful. I would be wracked with guilt."

CHAPTER 16

When we finished our run, I went home and baked some chocolate cupcakes for the officers down at the station. They were nothing fancy, just good old chocolate cupcakes, with a little sour cream added for moistness. And although there was nothing fancy about them, they turned out quite tasty, and I was rather pleased with them.

"Look what I've got," I announced as I walked through the front door of the police station. I was carrying two pink bakery boxes, each holding a dozen and a half of the chocolate cupcakes.

Jim Taylor sat at the front desk, and his eyes widened. "Oh, Allie, you have no idea how happy I am to see you."

I chuckled and brought the boxes to the front

desk. "I bet I can guess how happy you are. And I am so sorry that it's been a while since I've brought anything in for all of you wonderful officers."

He blushed. "Oh, that's all right. We're just thrilled when you have time to make something for us. Believe me, no one is complaining."

"Well, you are very welcome. I appreciate the job y'all do for this town." I lifted the lid on the top box. "You'd better grab a cupcake because once I put them in the break room, they're going to go fast."

He nodded and gently lifted one of the chocolate beauties from the box. "Look at that. That looks absolutely delicious. Allie, you are a kitchen magician."

I laughed. "No one has ever called me a kitchen magician before. I like it. And these are delicious, if I do say so myself. I had to taste test one, you know. Better grab another one. You don't want to miss out on these."

"You don't have to tell me twice. Thank you so much for making these, Allie."

I nodded and closed the lid after he took the second cupcake. "You are so welcome. I hope you enjoy them."

He grinned. "I will absolutely enjoy these."

I chuckled and picked up the boxes. "Can you buzz me through?"

"You bet." He hit the buzzer, and I carried the

cupcake boxes through the door leading to the offices.

I tapped on Alec's door with the toe of my shoe, and he hollered for me to come in. "I can't! I need you to open the door!" I called.

A moment later, he opened the door. When he saw what I was holding, he smiled. "Well, what do we have here?"

"Chocolate cupcakes. Nice, chocolaty, moist cupcakes. You'd better grab a couple for yourself before I put these in the break room."

"Don't mind if I do." He opened the top box and removed two of the cupcakes. "They smell incredible."

"I'll be right back." I hurried to the break room and set the boxes down on a table in the middle of the room. Three officers were taking a break, and when they caught sight of the bakery boxes, they hurried over.

"Enjoy yourselves, boys," I said and headed back to Alec's office.

He was sitting behind his desk, enjoying a cupcake. "This is so good."

I nodded. "Thanks. So, did Rebecca come in?" I had texted him to let him know earlier that she was supposed to stop in after her tennis game.

He nodded. "Yes, she told me what Penny had told her. I'll have another talk with Jonathan and

Dori, but I'm not sure if what she said seems substantial enough to warrant an investigation. The way she explained it, she thought Penny was being dramatic."

I sighed. "She told us that Penny told her she was worried about her husband harming her, and then she turned up dead. You don't think he had anything to do with her murder?"

He hesitated as he peeled the liner from his cupcake. "I'm not saying that he doesn't, but I'm not sure if what Penny was telling her really meant that she believed her husband was going to kill her." He looked at me. "I'm not going to dismiss what she's saying, but I just don't know yet. Something seems a bit off."

I nodded, taking this in. Alec had excellent instincts, so if he thought something was off, it probably was. "Would you like a cup of coffee with those cupcakes?"

He shook his head. "Not if you mean the stuff back in the break room. I don't want to sully the flavor of these delectable cupcakes with that stuff."

I chuckled. "Sully? Okay, we won't sully the flavor of the cupcakes. Did the lab get back to you with anything on the teacup?"

He gave a quick nod of his head and took another bite. When he had swallowed, he said, "Wow, you really outdid yourself with these, Allie. What's your secret?"

I shook my head. "A baker never reveals her secrets. Otherwise, who would I bake for? You could just make them for yourself."

He chuckled. "No way am I going to make them for myself. That's what I married you for."

I looked at him, one eyebrow raised. "Finally, the truth comes out."

He nodded and licked the chocolate frosting off his thumb. "Yep. There it is. I married you for your cupcakes. And your pies, cobblers, and tarts. And any other sweet, baked goodness that you create."

I chuckled and settled back in my seat. "I'm so glad you're a fan. Just think what would have happened if I had married somebody who didn't have a sweet tooth. I probably would get so depressed that I wouldn't bake anymore."

He stared at me wide-eyed. "I never thought of that. I'm doing you a service, so I deserve cupcakes more often."

I shook my head. "I doubt I'll make them more often than I already do. So, tell me, what about the results from the teacup? What did the lab say?"

He sighed. "Unfortunately, there were no traces of poison in that broken cup. There were fingerprints, but none of them were Penny's. Since there's no trace of poison, there's no point in running the prints to figure out who they belong to."

I groaned in disappointment. "I was so hoping that cup was going to answer questions for us. If it wasn't the one Penny was holding, I wonder how it ended up broken? Someone probably accidentally knocked it off the table, I guess," I answered myself. "So that leaves us with the question of who cleaned up the cup Penny was drinking from. Gemma said they didn't clean up until that afternoon, which was unfortunately before you and the other police officers arrived to investigate."

He nodded. "We don't really know if the poison was even in her tea. It could have been in something she ate earlier in the day."

"But the poison from Wolfsbane kicks in pretty quickly, so it couldn't have been consumed long before she collapsed. I looked it up. It's usually with an hour or so. There were so many people in the kitchen working to set up the party, and it seemed like someone would have noticed something. Did you talk to everyone?"

He nodded. "I talked to everybody on the guest list, as well as everyone who was working the party. No one saw anything unusual. And there wasn't much of anything in her stomach, so it very likely was given as a liquid. Tea is a very good guess, but there was coffee, iced tea, and two kinds of punch. The punch was brought by the caterer and the coffee and iced tea were made by two different people in the kitchen."

I brushed my hair away from my face. "And how did that plant end up on the patio? No one seems to know the answer to that question either. I'm assuming the killer had to have moved it there, but why? Why not just slip out to the garden and pluck a leaf or two and take it with them? Why move the entire plant to the patio?" This was one of those questions that was bothering me. It made more sense not to draw attention to the plant rather than bringing it to the patio, where anybody could have brushed up against it or even plucked a flower from it.

"Why even have one of those plants in your garden?" he asked. "Anybody could have accidentally been poisoned by it. The flowers are pretty, and somebody could have come along and picked some of them and been poisoned."

I shook my head. "It doesn't make sense, does it?"

"No. I wouldn't have allowed it on my property."

I thought about it for a few moments. "Somebody besides Penny knew it was a poisonous plant." I looked at him. "Arlene. Arlene told Lucy and me how poisonous the plant was. Who would have known otherwise?"

He rubbed his forehead. "Yes, Arlene knew about it, and she said she and Penny didn't have a good relationship. I hate to say it, but I probably need to talk to her again."

"It's tough thinking a little old lady might murder someone, isn't it?" I asked. "I certainly wouldn't want to think that's what happened."

He nodded and took another bite of his cupcake. "This is delicious. I'm so glad you stopped by today."

I nodded. "Me too. I just wish that teacup would have had some poison in it."

I sat back and watched him eat his cupcake. Arlene could easily have moved about the kitchen and poisoned something, then directed someone else to hand it to Penny. But how would she have moved the potted Wolfsbane to the patio by herself? It seemed like her cane would have made that impossible, or at the very least, difficult.

CHAPTER 17

The following morning, Lucy and I dropped by the Cup and Bean for some coffee and to see what Mr. Winters was up to. As we stood waiting for our coffees and our blueberry scones, I glanced over at the corner table and realized that Mr. Winters wasn't there. I elbowed Lucy, and when she looked at me, I nodded at the empty corner table.

"Well, would you look at that? I wonder where Mr. Winters is? I hope he's okay."

I nodded. "Me too." When you get used to something happening nearly every single day, you wonder about it when it doesn't. Mr. Winters was a man of habit, and his habit was to be here at the coffee shop, bright and early with Sadie, enjoying her pup cup. But he was also elderly, and we worried about him.

We got our coffee and scones and went over to the corner table, anyway. We both sat on the same side as we normally did, and I turned and looked at her. "I suppose we don't have to sit next to each other. You could sit across from me."

She shrugged. "This is my chair. I'm not moving."

I nodded. "Got it. It feels comfortable to sit in the same place every day, doesn't it?" We didn't come to the Cup and Bean *every* day, but I had to admit we were here frequently. Their coffee and baked goods were addicting, and I was an addict who wasn't looking to go into recovery.

"It sure does."

"Are you going to get the puppy?" I asked her and took a sip of my caramel delight iced latte. It had a generous amount of caramel, along with small caramel chips sprinkled on the whipped cream. Thank goodness I was a runner. Otherwise, all that caramel goodness was going to catch up with me.

She shook her head. "No, Ed says he's allergic to dogs. I think he might be lying."

I chuckled. "Do you think so?"

She nodded. "You know how he is. He's a stick in the mud."

"You should just adopt that puppy and bring her home as a surprise. He would fall in love with her and wouldn't complain."

She turned and looked at me with one eyebrow raised. "Have you met my husband? He's the king of complaining."

I laughed. "You've got a point." I took another sip of my iced coffee. It was delightful.

"What did I miss?"

We both looked up to see Mr. Winters standing in front of our table. Sadie trotted beneath the table and took up her regular seat.

"You didn't miss anything," I said. "Where have you been? You're late."

He nodded and laid his newspaper down on the table. "My alarm didn't go off." He shot Sadie a look under the table. "I think it was sabotaged." The little dog wagged her tail guiltily. "I've got to get my coffee and a pup cup. Be right back."

I turned to Lucy. "All is right with the world again."

She nodded. "Thank goodness."

Mr. Winters returned shortly with his black coffee and the pup cup for Sadie. He slipped it beneath the table and sat down across from us. "I've got news."

The look in his eyes said it was important. I leaned forward. "What? What did you find out?" I held my breath in anticipation.

He glanced around at the other people in the shop

before continuing. "I found out that Rebecca Adams and her husband are getting a divorce."

We stared at him for a moment, and I shook my head in disappointment. "And?"

He licked his lips before continuing. "And I found out that Rebecca was embezzling money from her husband's company. That's why he's divorcing her."

Lucy and I gasped. "Who embezzles money from their husband's company? That's thievery of the worst kind," Lucy said.

I nodded. "I can't imagine doing something like that to Alec. That's crazy."

He sighed and took a sip of his black coffee. "Isn't it, though? Who on earth would do such a thing?"

"What kind of company does her husband own?" I asked when it didn't immediately spring to mind.

"He owns a marketing company. From what I hear, he brings in a lot of money. He's very good at what he does, apparently. Rebecca occasionally worked for him when she got bored, and I guess she took that opportunity to steal money from him."

I shook my head. "Why on earth would she do that? Oh, wait a minute. She owns a very expensive SUV. It was parked in the driveway."

Lucy nodded. "Yes, I think those vehicles sell for at least a hundred grand. But wouldn't her husband wonder where she was getting the money from? I mean, you don't drive one of those cars home without your husband noticing."

"That's exactly right," I said. "He should have known she had a whole lot of money at her disposal. Who did you find this out from?"

Mr. Winters leaned in. "Bella Davis. She's Rebecca's niece, and she's engaged to my neighbor's son. We were talking this morning, and she told me about the embezzlement and their divorce. But you know the Adams's, they have a lot of money. I really don't know why she did it."

"Maybe she wanted to leave him, and she was saving up the money to do it," I suggested.

"That could be," Lucy said. "If she was afraid she wouldn't get much in the divorce, she may have been taking her own little stash of cash."

Mr. Winters took a sip of his coffee. "My neighbor says that Rebecca likes everything that's expensive. She won't go for anything cheap. Her clothes are designer, her shoes are designer, and she has the most expensive furniture she can get her hands on. So, it's not surprising that she has a vehicle that's as pricey as you say."

I took a bite of my scone, taking this in. How embarrassing to be caught stealing from your spouse.

Humiliating even. But if she had access to their regular bank accounts, why would she need to steal? I looked at Mr. Winters, about to ask that question, when he said, "Apparently, her husband keeps a tight rein on the finances, but she somehow finds money to spend. She used to be a lawyer, you know, so I'm sure she had her own money that she saved, but she's a big-time spender."

I shrugged. "Okay, so she steals from her husband. Still, you would think that he would notice all of those things she was buying if she insisted on the best of everything. How could he be keeping a tight rein on the money if she's always spending?"

He shrugged. "I'm sure she has money of her own to spend. But maybe her husband didn't have as tight of a rein on the money as he thought he did. Maybe she was lying about how much she spent on things so he wouldn't catch on."

I nodded. "I guess that's possible, but you would think he would figure it out."

"Yeah, Ed isn't aware of how much money I spend, but if I started bringing in fur coats or expensive vehicles, you can bet he would catch on and say something about it," Lucy said.

"Did your neighbor say how long it's been since they decided they're getting a divorce?" I asked him.

"Has it been in the works for a while? Or is this something new?"

"It's something new. He told her to pack her things and get out two days ago." He took a sip of his coffee.

"Wow," I said. "So, she's going to lose her home, too? Why does she have to be the one who has to leave?"

"Because she's the thief," Lucy said, nodding.

"But doesn't it have to be proven in court that she was embezzling?" I asked. "I can't imagine that she would just admit to him she had done it. I bet she's going to lie and maintain her innocence."

Mr. Winters shrugged. "She might do that, but maybe he caught her red-handed. Maybe the evidence he has is so condemning that she can't lie her way out of it."

I sighed. "The trials and tribulations of the wealthy."

Lucy nodded. "Right? I heard years ago that Roger Adams's business was doing very well, and from the looks of things, they've never been hurting for money. Still, it had to be devastating for him to have figured out that she was stealing from him. I would hate to be in his position."

"That's true," I agreed. "What an awful betrayal."

Mr. Winters took a sip of his coffee and grimaced.

"It's an awful thing, isn't it? Some people just aren't trustworthy."

I would never have thought that Rebecca Adams would steal from her husband. It was a shame she felt the need to do it. The betrayal was definitely something that would be hard to get past, and I didn't blame her husband one bit for wanting a divorce.

CHAPTER 18

"It's a shame about Rebecca and her husband," Lucy said as we ran.

I nodded, trying to keep my breathing steady. This neighborhood had gently rolling hills, but they were deceiving. They were harder to run than we had first thought. "It really is. But if Rebecca embezzled from her husband, you can't blame him. I wouldn't want to be married to somebody who was stealing from me."

She nodded and inhaled. "No, you can't blame him at all. It's all on her if she really did it. Do you think she did? It just doesn't seem like something a woman like Rebecca would do."

I glanced at her. "You mean because she's rich?"

She nodded. "Sure, she's got everything she could ever want, so why does she need to steal? And especially from her husband. It doesn't make sense, does it?"

I shook my head. "No, it doesn't make sense." I didn't know Rebecca well enough to know if she would steal from her husband. But Lucy was right. She didn't seem like the kind of person who would do that. If you have access to all the money in the world, why do you need to steal more? But some people are never satisfied with what they have, no matter how much it is.

My calves were burning as we ran up another hill. "I'm not sure this was the best neighborhood to run in today. I didn't get as much sleep as I should have last night."

"We can walk for a bit if you want," she said hopefully.

I grinned. "That's not a bad idea." We slowed to a walk. "There, my body is going to appreciate this much more than the running."

She nodded. "Mine too. Does Alec have any more leads on Penny's murder?"

I shook my head. "No, we were really putting our hopes on that teacup. I sure would like to know who cleaned up the broken teacup and who moved that plant onto the patio."

"Me too. It had to be the killer, but why? Why move the plant like that?"

I shook my head as we walked, trying to steady my breathing again. It was a beautiful day for a run, and I enjoyed mornings like this. We probably would have been better off running on the trail, though, as it was reasonably flat and well-paved.

"Did you notice at the party that Penny wasn't very nice to Rebecca?" I asked.

She thought about it for a moment as we walked. "I remember she said something to her about whether she was just going to stand there, and she didn't say it nicely."

I nodded, thinking about it. "Maybe Penny was just stressed out about the party."

"Probably so." She took a sip from her water bottle.

We walked along in silence for several minutes, and then I remembered something Rebecca had said. "Rebecca said she and Penny told each other everything. She emphasized it was everything."

"Well, we tell each other everything, don't we?" She turned to look at me.

I nodded. "Yes, we do. But one of us isn't embezzling from her husband. At least, I don't think she is," I said, glancing at her.

She chuckled. "No, one of us is not embezzling from her husband, mostly because her husband doesn't have any money to embezzle."

I laughed. "Mine either. Or at least not enough to embezzle from him."

After another couple of minutes of walking in silence, Lucy glanced at me. "What are you trying to say?"

I shook my head. "I'm not sure, but that sure is an expensive vehicle that Rebecca drives." I turned to her. "Let's go down this block." We made a right and broke into a slow jog for four more blocks and then made a left. Rebecca's home was just ahead.

As we approached the house, I noticed the SUV sitting in the driveway again. "If I had a vehicle that expensive, I wouldn't want to leave it out in the driveway like that. You never know when somebody might be up to no good and might damage it or steal it." We came to a stop at the end of her driveway.

She nodded. "Yeah, I would keep a fancy vehicle like that in the garage at all times. I mean, when I'm not driving it, anyway."

"I wonder what she's got in the garage that keeps this vehicle outside." We stopped in her driveway, admiring the SUV.

"Oh, I didn't think about that. I wonder if what's in the garage makes this SUV look like a second-hand vehicle," she said.

"It just might." I hadn't seen Rebecca driving

around town, so I didn't know if this was her only vehicle or if she had another.

"I thought her husband told her she had to move out?" Lucy pointed out.

I nodded. "Maybe he kept the vehicle as payment for what she took."

"That's a good idea. If she did steal money from him, he's going to want it back."

As we stood there talking, Rebecca suddenly opened her front door and stepped out onto her porch. She was dressed to play tennis again, and when she saw us, a puzzled look crossed her face. "Well, good morning, ladies. Fancy meeting you here."

I smiled. "Good morning, Rebecca. We were just going for a run in the neighborhood, and we thought we would stop by and take a rest. These hills are steeper than they look, or we're not in as good of shape as we thought we were." I laughed.

"We thought you wouldn't mind if we rested in your driveway and caught our breath," Lucy explained.

Rebecca nodded, smiled, and locked her front door, then headed down the porch steps. "Oh, of course not. You ladies take as long as you like. I've got to get to the country club to play tennis. I love getting up and going early. It just makes my day."

When she got closer to us, I could see her eyes looked puffy and red. "How are you doing, Rebecca?"

She hesitated. "I am really missing Penny. I wish she were here to talk to."

I nodded. "I'm sure that's one of the hardest things about losing your best friend. Not having her to talk things over with. I know you said that the two of you told each other everything, so this has got to be so hard for you."

A puzzled look crossed her face again for just a moment, and then she smiled. "Yes, who do you talk to when you want to talk about those intimate things you don't want the world to know about and your best friend is gone? I don't have a clue. Penny and I would often brew a pot of tea and sit and chat about everything. Penny loved her tea. I swear, the more bitter it tasted, the more she enjoyed it." She chuckled. "Personally, I don't like it as strong and bitter as she took it, but she would always insist that I make that pot of tea for her when she came to visit. It was the least I could do, so I made it for her. But Penny was my sounding board, and now she's gone. I feel so lost."

I nodded. "I'm so sorry. What you're going through really needs to be talked over with someone you can trust."

She stared at me. "What I'm going through?"

I nodded. "Yes, I'm sure that a divorce is really hard to get through with no one to talk to."

Her mouth dropped open. "Divorce? What are you talking about?"

I shook my head. "Oh gosh, did I speak out of turn? I'm sorry. Someone mentioned you were getting divorced. I shouldn't have said anything. I'm so sorry." I watched closely for her reaction to what I had just said, and I wasn't disappointed.

Her mouth closed, her face going pale, and then she stared at me for an uncomfortable moment. "Who told you that?"

I shook my head, glancing at Lucy. "I don't really remember who said it. I thought it was common knowledge. Forgive me for saying anything. I'm sorry Penny isn't here to help you through this."

Her brow furrowed. "Penny was rather opinionated about a lot of things that I brought up with her. She would be opinionated about this, too." She crossed her arms in front of herself. "I don't know who's been spreading rumors about me, but yes, Roger and I are indeed getting a divorce. It isn't anybody's business, though."

"Did Penny know that you sometimes helped yourself to Roger's business?" I asked. It was a cruel thing to say, but I suddenly saw what had to have happened between the two so-called friends. Penny knew all about her thieving friend and she made her pay for it.

Her eyes widened. "What? What are you talking about? Helped myself to Roger's business?"

"Yes, you helped yourself to his business, didn't you?" Lucy asked. I didn't know if she had caught on to what I now understood, but she was going to play along. That's what friends are for.

Rebecca's mouth dropped open. "I don't know what you two are talking about. If you'll excuse me, I've got to be going." She dug in her purse for her keys.

"That's a beautiful SUV," I said. "Lucy and I were just admiring it. But they're so expensive. There's no way either of us could ever afford to buy one of those."

She nodded. "I say if you're going to get something, then get the best. It pays to invest in quality. I've got to get going now. Have a good day."

"Did your husband pay for it? And did he know he was paying for it?" I asked.

She narrowed her eyes at me. "Allie, I don't know why you're saying these things, but I have to go now." She went around to the driver's side and then turned back to me. "I don't know what you've got in your head, but you're wrong. Penny was my best friend, and I cared about her."

"You cared enough to make her some poisoned tea, didn't you?" I asked. "I bet she couldn't even taste the poison over the bitterness she enjoyed in her tea."

Her mouth dropped open. "How dare you! You have no right to say those things about me! I would never have poisoned Penny. I'm not saying that she didn't deserve it, but I would never do that to her. Because, even though we were best friends, she could be incredibly cruel. She may have thought she was better than me and that she could force me to do whatever she wanted, but she was wrong. And that does not mean that I poisoned her." She got into her SUV and started it, and Lucy and I got out of the way as she put it in reverse and gunned it. I called Alec and told him about the tea and the embezzled money.

CHAPTER 19

"Dixie, I'm getting sleepy."

Dixie was sitting in my lap, and he looked up at me, his eyes half-closed. He turned up the volume on his purring and laid his head back down on his paws. Apparently, Dixie was also getting tired.

Alec had texted me earlier that Rebecca was caught five miles outside of town. She knew the jig was up and she was leaving. I heard the key in the door and sighed. It was the middle of the night, and Alec was home.

A moment later he stood in the living room doorway and smiled tiredly. "Well, what do we have here?"

"A very tired wife and cat." Dixie raised his head and meowed.

He chuckled and came to sit next to me on the couch. Leaning over, he kissed me and scratched Dixie's head. "You didn't need to wait up."

"I didn't need to, but I wanted to. So, spill it. Give me all the details."

He laid his head on my shoulder. "Rebecca finally confessed to murdering Penny. All these years, she swore Penny was her best friend, and she could tell her anything."

"But she made the mistake of telling her she was embezzling from her husband's business, didn't she?" I had figured that part out after putting the pieces of the puzzle together. There are some people you simply can't tell your secrets to.

He nodded. "She was so pleased with herself. She was certain that her husband would never catch on. But sadly, she made a mistake and took too much money from the account. Roger had been suspicious that something was going on for months, but it wasn't until Rebecca overplayed her hand that he finally figured it out."

"Cheaters never prosper," I said, petting Dixie.

"They certainly don't."

"So, what happened between her and Penny?"

He sat up. "Penny decided she wanted in on the action. She told Rebecca she was going to tell Roger that she was embezzling from his company if she didn't give her a cut of the money."

I shook my head. "So, Penny was blackmailing her."

"Yes, she was blackmailing her, and Rebecca was tired of it. She decided that the only way she could get out of this mess was to kill Penny because she did not want her husband to know what she was doing. She knew Penny had the Wolfsbane plant in her garden, so she pinched off some leaves and made a tea out of it, adding it to Penny's tea."

"How was she certain that only Penny would drink it?" I asked. "Do you want some cocoa? Something to eat?"

He shook his head. "No, I'm fine. Rebecca was in the kitchen helping Penny oversee the preparations. She said Penny was becoming stressed about the garden party, so she made her a cup of tea. And having already made the Wolfsbane into a tea at her house, she poured just enough of the poison into a small vial, and while making the tea for Penny, she dumped it into the cup and handed it to Penny herself. She stood nearby to be sure that Penny would drink it, and she did."

"Interesting," I said. "So why was the plant on the patio? If the plant hadn't ended up there, it might have taken us longer to figure out what she died from. I mean, the toxicology report would come out eventually, but we were fairly sure she had been poisoned with the Wolfsbane from the very beginning."

"She brought it to the patio hoping that it would seem that there was no way to tell who could have used it to murder Penny. There were a lot of guests at the party, and it could have been anyone. At least that's what she hoped we would believe."

"Ah. Misdirection. I like it. But someone would have to have a reason to kill her, so it couldn't have been just anyone," I pointed out.

He nodded. "Exactly."

"Why wasn't there any poison in the teacup?" I asked. "Was it the same teacup Penny was drinking from when she collapsed?"

He shook his head. "It wasn't the same teacup. After everyone had left the house, Rebecca stayed behind and picked up the broken teacup. Then she broke another teacup and left it there on the patio so that everyone would think it was the one Penny had been drinking out of. No poison in the teacup, no poisoned tea."

I smiled. "Oh, that was a clever move. Or at least it would have been a clever move if she hadn't been greedy and stolen too much money from her husband's business. It might have taken us a lot longer to put everything together if she hadn't done that. Thank goodness people like to gossip in this town or we might not have heard about Rebecca's divorce for months."

He chuckled. "Yes, she was far too greedy, and thank goodness for those busybodies."

I yawned and stretched. "Why don't we go up to bed?"

"That's a great idea." He leaned over and kissed me, and I set Dixie on the floor. We went upstairs.

It was a shame that Penny couldn't keep her own greed at bay and hadn't blackmailed Rebecca. She might still have been alive if she hadn't. Neither of these women were satisfied with what they already had, and their greed got the best of them.

I'd call Lucy in the morning and fill her in, because that's what best friends are for.

The End

Sign up to receive my newsletter for updates on new releases and sales:

https://www.subscribepage.com/kathleen-suzette

Follow me on Facebook:

https://www.facebook.com/Kathleen-Suzette-Kate-Bell-authors-759206390932120

BOOKS BY KATHLEEN SUZETTE:

A PUMPKIN HOLLOW CANDY STORE MYSTERY

Treats, Tricks, and Trespassing
Gumdrops, Ghosts, and Graveyards
Confections, Clues, and Chocolate

A FRESHLY BAKED COZY MYSTERY SERIES

Apple Pie a la Murder
Trick or Treat and Murder
Thankfully Dead
Candy Cane Killer
Ice Cold Murder
Love is Murder
Strawberry Surprise Killer
Plum Dead
Red, White, and Blue Murder
Mummy Pie Murder
Wedding Bell Blunders
In a Jam
Tarts and Terror
Fall for Murder
Web of Deceit

A FRESHLY BAKED COZY MYSTERY SERIES

Silenced Santa
New Year, New Murder
Murder Supreme
Peach of a Murder
Sweet Tea and Terror
Die for Pie
Gnome for Halloween
Christmas Cake Caper
Valentine Villainy
Cupcakes and Beaches
Cinnamon Roll Secrets
Pumpkin Pie Peril
Dipped in Murder
A Pinch of Homicide
Layered Lies

A COOKIE'S CREAMERY MYSTERY

Ice Cream, You Scream
Murder with a Cherry on top
Murderous 4th of July
Murder at the Shore
Merry Murder
A Scoop of Trouble
Lethal Lemon Sherbet
Berry Deadly Delight
Chilled to the Cone

A LEMON CREEK MYSTERY

Murder at the Ranch
The Art of Murder
Body on the Boat

A Pumpkin Hollow Mystery Series

Candy Coated Murder
Murderously Sweet
Chocolate Covered Murder
Death and Sweets
Sugared Demise
Confectionately Dead
Hard Candy and a Killer
Candy Kisses and a Killer
Terminal Taffy

Fudgy Fatality
Truffled Murder
Caramel Murder
Peppermint Fudge Killer
Chocolate Heart Killer
Strawberry Creams and Death
Pumpkin Spice Lies
Sweetly Dead
Deadly Valentine
Death and a Peppermint Patty
Sugar, Spice, and Murder
Candy Crushed
Trick or Treat
Frightfully Dead
Candied Murder
Christmas Calamity

A RAINEY DAYE COZY MYSTERY SERIES

Clam Chowder and a Murder
A Short Stack and a Murder
Cherry Pie and a Murder
Barbecue and a Murder
Birthday Cake and a Murder
Hot Cider and a Murder
Roast Turkey and a Murder
Gingerbread and a Murder
Fish Fry and a Murder
Cupcakes and a Murder
Lemon Pie and a Murder
Pasta and a Murder
Chocolate Cake and a Murder
Pumpkin Spice Donuts and a Murder

A RAINEY DAYE COZY MYSTERY SERIES

Christmas Cookies and a Murder
Lollipops and a Murder
Picnic and a Murder
Wedding Cake and a Murder

Printed in Great Britain
by Amazon